Lumberjacks in Love

Sugar Maple

Apple Pine

Jacqueline Carmine

Contents

Sugar Maple

Jacqueline Carmine

Tobias

Before the sun is up, I'm out of bed and dressed. The flannel shirt and the worn jeans combo has served me well over the last decade. The lumberyard takes most of my focus on a daily basis, but it's not pine and oak that has me crawling out of bed at such an ungodly hour.

My father handed off the lumberyard to me and my brothers last year. He's focused on wood carvings, football, and rebuilding a 1965 Ford Mustang in that order. But it's not the administrative responsibilities I have now dragging me out of bed.

It's my mother. Or to be more accurate mother's bakery. *Sugar Crossing* is her legacy. She grew up in Crescent Ridge and founded her bakery well before my father ever came through as a traveling construction worker. I may be the eldest son but all three of us know that the bakery is really her baby. Her first born.

By all rights, my mother should be retired with my father. Taking up a hobby like crocheting or knitting. Instead, she continues to wake up at three every morning to bake bread, cookies, pies, and rolls before she opens. Sam is helping, but my mother needs to hire more hands.

It's why I'm driving down the mountain towards Main Street rather than up to the lumberyard or even better staying in my toasty warm bed.

It's full dark, my headlights are the only light source. We have a fresh coating of snow, and the tires of my four-wheel drive truck are cutting a fresh line through the white dusting. I go slow keeping an eye out for elk as they like to cross through in the early hours.

I park my truck next to my father's square body Chevy. Since his retirement he's insisted that my mother take it to work. There's nothing wrong with her all-wheel drive SUV but I know he worries all the same. Never mind that they could walk to the bakery from their cabin.

"Toby sweetheart," my mother calls as I stomp the snow from my boots by the front door. "I wasn't expecting you today."

Of course she wasn't. I swore yesterday would be the last day I would help at the bakery. Just like the day before and the day before that. I greet her with a kiss on her plump cheek, but I don't address her comment. We both know that I'm not going to leave my mother to sort all her orders and prep a full day's work by herself. She can fool my father and my brothers she can't fool me.

The arthritis in her wrists is getting worse every year and I know kneading the dough is becoming especially painful for her. The worker she hired a few years back is the same age as my youngest brother and I suspect she's noticed as well because she has started taking an earlier shift with more hours in an effort to alleviate my mother's burden.

As if she can read my thoughts my mother says, "I'm retiring."

It's nothing she hasn't said before, so I don't immediately respond. She pulls out a tray of bread loaves from the proofing oven.

"I'm serious," she says. "I got a sign in the window and an ad in the newspaper. I don't want to sell the bakery, but I do want to step back and hire a full-time baker."

All this is well and good, but I'll believe it when I see it.

"Swing by later," she says as she rolls a cart full of sourdough and rye bread into the walk-in oven. "I'm doing interviews, and I'd love to get your feedback because I know you're a good judge of character."

Promptly at six my mother flips the sign on the front door to open and I leave just as her first customers walk in the door. The Jergens always stop by for a morning muffin on their way to the coffee shop.

On my way back up the mountain to the lumberyard I can appreciate the beauty that kept my mother in Crescent Ridge all her life. I did my fair share of traveling in my twenties, even went off to college and earned a business degree down in Denver but much like my mother I don't see how I could ever leave my small hometown.

Six hours later and the crew is breaking for lunch. My brothers pull out packed lunches, but I can't resist the temptation to see if my mother is actually going to follow through with her plan. Sam is working today, and I know she'll tell me if my mother actually arranged any interviews.

Customers fill every table, nibbling on muffins, scones, or cookies and there is a short line to the register where Sam is taking and filling orders. The same as any other day the only difference is that my mother is not behind the counter with Sam making small talk with all her regulars.

I wave to the blonde girl as I step around the corner of the counter and walk through the door separating the prep area from the storefront. I have to turn sideways to let a petite redhead pass by as she stomps out of the back office. My mother's round face lights up with a smile when I enter her office. She's wearing her wire frame glasses and I can see from the stack of paper sitting on her desk that she is indeed collecting resumes and conducting interviews.

"Any luck yet?" I ask.

"Not yet," she replies. "None are a good fit for our family."

I'm about to comment that the baker just needs to be good at their craft when Sam knocks on the open door and sticks her head in.

"Elaine there's a woman out front who saw your sign and would like to know about the baker position."

"Send her back," my mother replies quickly. "Tobias sit in on this one, will you?"

It's not a request. She's patting the comically small stool she's stuck in the corner for when us kids got out of school early and kept her company.

I ignore the stool in favor of leaning against the wall in the corner. This isn't my business and while I know more about baking than most this needs to be my mother's decision. I don't want to influence her process.

"Hello," a sugar sweet voice calls from the door.

Even as my mother greets the woman her silver hair a stark contrast to the maple brown curls, I'm embarrassed to find my cock taking notice of the woman. She's not a local or I would recognize her. Her curls are in a neat ponytail that's long enough to have her hair drape over her shoulder. Perky breasts hide underneath a T-shirt emblazoned with *Crescent Ridge Trail Rides* and I fight back a groan.

She's a tourist. The hottest woman I've seen in my life and of course she's a tourist. No way is she actually here for an interview. Must be here to compliment my mother's baking.

"Hello sweetheart," my mother replies.

She shoots me a quick glance but even if I wanted to be polite and greet the woman I couldn't. My tongue sticks to the roof of my mouth as if glued, even as my eyes rake over her curves. It's been a long time since I've gotten bent out of shape over a woman. And never to such a degree that I couldn't speak.

Her eyes are a dark shade of brown with a warm ring of caramel around the pupil. The kind of eyes I wouldn't mind looking at first thing in the morning.

I shift in place, crossing my ankles as I do so that the bulge I'm trying to hide isn't obvious. There is an odd mix of sawdust and flour on my shirt, my jeans worn from repeated washings, and my steel toe is beginning to show through the leather of my boots. Everything about me is at odds with the woman in front of me.

Her nails are fake. Long and studded with gems, the exact shade reminds me of the evergreens that surround the ridge. The way her leggings hug her thighs threatens to send me spiraling as she greets my mother while shooting me a shy glance.

"Carina Rutler."

Damn shame that she's a tourist.

Carina

"Elaine Carmichael," the petite woman says as I shake her hand. "And this is my oldest son, Tobias. Don't mind him. Without a wife of his own to fret over he's reduced to worrying over me."

The man attempting to squish himself into the corner looks mildly embarrassed by his mother's words but doesn't offer a hand in introduction, so I try not to stare at the muscles straining his clothing. If the bulging biceps testing the red flannel weren't enough, his jeans are tighter than mine and I've always been a fan of thunder thighs.

It takes conscious effort to focus on the woman and not the gruff man lingering like a shadow. A delicious shadow with forest green eyes that threatens to steal my sanity even as I ramble on about how much I love their quaint little town.

There is no chance Elaine is going to give me a job in her bakery. I have zero experience with bread, and I don't even have a permanent residence in town. I'm the literal definition of a wild card gamble and that is the reddest of red flags to a small business owner.

Still, she talks to me for the better part of an hour. Her smile never falters even when she asks Tobias a question and he just grunts and grumbles in response. She is too sweet to have such a grumpy son. With her silver hair pinned neatly into a bun and her round figure she looks remarkably similar to Mrs. Claus.

"So, you're staying in Crescent Ridge then?" she asks after a while.

It's a valid question. One I've been holding close to my heart ever since I drove down Main to the *Firefly Inn*. There's something magical about this town, something that makes me feel relaxed and at peace, as if I've lived here my entire life.

Cassandra had her wedding here at the resort that overlooks the Viridian Mountains. It was a beautiful ceremony, and she deserved her happily ever after. Best friends since first grade I was happy to serve as her maid of honor. But now with Cassandra and her husband, Mitch, on their honeymoon and all our friends departing back to their homes that magic is still with me.

I don't want to leave. Something is calling to me and I feel more at home here than I ever did in Denver. With

Cassandra moving to Texas with her husband and my parents gone there is nothing holding me to the mile high city.

"I want to," I tell her.

It's the only thing I can say because there are so many moving pieces involved in this spur of the moment decision. Except it doesn't feel impulsive. It feels right, like I'm finally where I'm meant to be.

"Can you start tomorrow?" she asks. "Bright and early at three in the morning."

For a second her words don't hit me and I'm afraid I sit there across from her desk with my jaw popped open in shock.

"Absolutely!" I shout. "Two-thirty even."

Her tinkling laugh is surprisingly loud in the small office.

"Three will do just fine," she says. "We'll have you trained in no time."

I leave *Sugar Crossing* with a spring in my step. By the time I get back to my room at the *Firefly Inn* I have the makings of a plan. There are four apartments for rent in town and two are well within my price range and immediately available. One quick tour later and I'm signing my brand-new lease. A quick phone call to my landlord to give notice and another to schedule a moving truck for the following weekend and I am officially well on my way to becoming a Crescent Ridge local.

The next morning, I arrive promptly, and Elaine's welcoming smile is just as warm and genuine as it was yesterday. No grumpy son in sight but I would be lying if I said the man wasn't on my mind for most of the night.

I never even heard his voice. But that doesn't mean his image isn't burned into my mind's eye.

***

"Elaine..."

The skin around her mouth is tight as she turns to face me. Her smile fixed in place. Apparently, there is more to baking than hard work. There is skill and precision, and I have neither. Add in the nerves and the self-imposed pressure to do well and I'm not only falling short but I'm making careless mistakes.

First, I lost one of my nails in the bread dough and we scrapped every batch I worked on. Dozens of loaves straight into the trash. Elaine couldn't risk selling them to even her most loyal and forgiving customers since it was a safety risk. Then I mixed up the salt and the sugar for the chocolate chip cookie recipe and made the most awful and inedible batch of salty cookies ever created.

The only highlight of my morning was meeting Samantha, a woman five years younger than me who prefers to go by Sam. She's the same blonde who I asked about the sign in the window yesterday and she is a fountain of optimism despite my numerous setbacks. But now she's handling the counter out front while Elaine is trying to teach me the basics of baking.

Elaine picks up one of the snickerdoodles I just pulled out of the oven and not even the sweet old woman can hide her disgust.

"Ginger instead of cinnamon," she tells me with a shake of her head. "It's a common mistake."

That's what she says every time I mess up. I'm getting fired by the time I leave today.

"Tell you what," Elaine begins, and I brace for the blow. "Why don't you take a breather? I'll send you up to the lumberyard where Tobias and his brothers work with some biscuits and honey. It'll help you get out of your head and relax."

She's pushing a wicker basket lined with a linen cloth and filled with buttermilk biscuits into my hands before I can find my voice to respond. Maybe she's sending me up to see her son so that she doesn't have to fire me. I bet he handles that part of the business because she seems far too sweet to fire anyone.

"Smile sweetheart," she tells me on the way to my car. "It's just your first day and we all have to start somewhere."

I'm glad she wrote the directions down on a napkin because my phone lost the GPS signal halfway up the mountain. The roads all have curves and switchbacks with hand painted wooden signs. Some are faded and almost illegible.

Finally, just when I think I'm well and utterly lost, I see the sign for the *Carmichael Lumberyard*. I park next to a row of trucks. Some are old and some are brand new, but every single one is four-wheel drive. If I'm really staying in Crescent Ridge I might need to invest in a new set of wheels before winter.

Barely out of the car, a man shouts, and I turn to see someone who could only be another of Elaine's sons.

Taller than Tobias he has a lean frame with curly dark hair peeking out from underneath a worn blue baseball hat. Wearing a T-shirt that has faded from washing he has his jeans tucked into his brown leather square toed cowboy boots.

His frown melts into a smile when he sees the wicker basket I pull out of the backseat.

"Mama sent you with treats?" he asks.

On his heels is a shorter man with short dirty blonde hair and an infectious grin.

"You must be Carina," the second man says. "Mom said you were on your way with biscuits. I'm Everett and this chipmunk is Jonathan."

He jerks his thumb at his brother who is taking a bite of a biscuit despite his cheek bulging out from his previous bite. Chipmunk indeed.

"Nice to meet you," I reply.

Three more men have joined the circle surrounding my car and they all introduce themselves before taking a biscuit. Buzz is an older bald man who has a wad of chewing tobacco that causes him to spit every five minutes and is missing three fingers on one hand. Farmer Dan is barely out of high school and wears a straw hat. And the last man, Casanova, is a ridiculous over the top flirt.

"Is it hot out here or is it just you?" he asks the second he sees me.

"Um," I say.

"Sweetheart your lips look lonely. Would they like to meet mine?" he tries again with a wide grin on his face.

"Garrett!" a loud voice booms.

The other men scatter as Everett smirks and Jonathan rolls his eyes in annoyance.

"Wha-" Casanova whose actual name is Garrett turns to see Tobias storming towards him and abruptly decides he has better places to be.

Tobias approaches, his long strides eating up the remaining distance between us as his brothers murmur their farewells before their thundercloud of a brother arrives.

Jonathan takes two more biscuits with a promise not to feed the squirrels, but I don't have time to think about his odd comment. Tobias is looming over me. His clothes are sprinkled with sawdust, and he smells like sweat and pine. If it weren't for his frown I would melt into a puddle of goo at his feet. All the raw masculinity on display threatens to turn me into a simpering idiot.

Tobias

"What are you doing here?" I ask.

The woman my mother hired, Carina, turns to look up at me with her big brown eyes open wide. Maybe it's my curt tone or maybe she always looks like a startled bunny. I don't know and I don't care.

She's distracting the men. If the machinery doesn't run, we don't make money. To come over and find that lecherous punk attempting to pick her up while he's supposed to be working was just the cherry topped nail in the coffin that is my day.

"Your mother sent me," she replies.

I spy the wicker basket she's holding and nearly groan. No doubt my mother didn't tell her about the particular history behind that basket. Everett and Jonathan both took notice judging by the twin smirks plastered on their faces when they sauntered by on their way back to work.

To Carina, it's just a basket but to my mother it's a tradition. The Carmichael Courting Basket. A tradition passed down through the women of our family. It's given to sons, daughters, and occasionally prospective brides as a sign of motherly approval.

Mother is meddling.

I knew it was too good to be true that she was looking for a replacement baker. Everett pried Sam for details and found out that our mother was only interviewing female candidates. Everyone but me knew that my mother was hunting for a bride. Not just anyone's bride. Mine.

I'm the only brother without any prospects. Anyone who has seen Everett and Sam interact knows that my youngest brother is smitten with his best friend. Jonathan on the other hand can't stop staring at the woman who delivers supplies each week.

Despite knowing all this I don't send her back down the mountain.

"Let's eat inside," I say jerking my thumb over my shoulder to indicate the single wide trailer that serves as our administrative office.

Carina follows me as I lead the way across the muddy lot. We constantly have heavy equipment moving through so there is no grass and there are tracks from the large wheels imprinted in the mud. She was smiling while talking with my brothers and the other men but the second I showed up her smile faded.

The trailer isn't anything special. One large open space with three desks, a small kitchenette, and a bathroom.

"Have a seat." I gesture to the round laminated table that wobbles.

Fetching a pair of water bottles from the mini fridge behind my desk I return to find Carina has set out the biscuits and the honey, blackberry jam, and homemade butter. Once you go homemade you can never go back to store bought.

"Just get it over with," she says with a forlorn sigh.

My brows furrow as I consider her defeated attitude. Color me intrigued.

"Get what over with?" I ask.

She shoots me an irritated look. All narrowed eyes and pursed lips. The sharp and flinty glare would cut a weaker man.

"Firing me," she replies. "I know that's why I'm here. Elaine is way too nice and it's absurdly clear that you handle the dirty work for her. Get. It. Over. With."

The amusement is clear on my face, as she smothers the biscuit in front of her with butter and jam in equal amounts. She doesn't look at me as she takes her first bite. Not even the fluffy layers can smother the pleased moan she lets out.

"You're not fired," I tell her.

Her brown eyes snap to mine.

"I'm not my mother's boogeyman," I add before letting out an amused chuckle. "That's my father's role. He ran this lumberyard for over thirty years, and he would have no problem sending you packing."

At the corner of her mouth there is a tiny crumb.

"Do you?" she asks.

Her question snaps my focus back to her eyes. She's looking at me expectantly, but I've lost the train of conversation.

"Hm?" I ask.

"Do you have a problem firing me?"

She can't be serious.

I've been staring at her since she waltzed into the bakery's office. Even Jonathan noticed my obsession and he's so food motivated I'm surprised he noticed it at all. He better not be feeding the squirrels again.

"Do you enjoy baking?" I ask instead of answering her question.

"No," she admits. "My mother didn't bake so I never learned growing up and I thought it would be easy. Funny how wrong I was."

"None of us learned either and obviously our mother *does* bake."

Her answering smile doesn't budge the flaky crumb and my resolve is weakening. My hand reaches out as she's telling me about a classic salt and sugar mix up and her words trail off.

The crumb falls away from her cheek, but my hand doesn't drop. With her eyes on mine and my hand caressing her soft skin I can't think straight. Like iron pulled to a magnet I find myself leaning closer until our lips meet.

Carina's lips are pliable under mine the sweet taste of jam and butter lingering on her tongue as we kiss. I'm ready to toss the remaining biscuits and the basket, family heirloom be damned, to the side to clear my way to her when the storm door bangs open, and we jump apart.

Her hair is mussed, her cheeks are cherry red and I'm sure that I'm in a similar state.

"Busted," Everett says with a shit eating grin.

I think that's going to be the end of it but then he leans out of the open doorway and hollers to our brother.

"Tobias has a girlfriend!"

He's only five years younger than me but sometimes that gap seems too small. At twenty-five I was certainly less of a jackass.

"That cute little baker?" Jonathan hollers back.

Carina's palms slam down on the tan laminate of the table, and she jumps up with purpose.

"Well," she says. "I need to get back to work!"

She brushes past my brothers without a word, the wicker basket tucked tightly to her chest like a shield. I follow in her wake, shoving Everett into the door on my way.

"Oi!" he shouts.

I ignore him in favor of catching up to the woman running away from me. Just barely beating her to the car, she doesn't look at me as I open the door for her. That won't do.

"Hey," I say. "You're fired."

Her chin jerks up as her rage filled eyes meet mine. The soft brown morphing into a cold and unforgiving shade closer to black as she starts to argue.

"Joking," I say tugging on her curly ponytail. "I just wanted you to look at me again."

She softens, her shoulders relax and before I can ask her to dinner, she's stretching up onto her toes and pressing her lips to mine. Wet and slippery she keeps this kiss short and I'm still standing dazed as she packs up her car and leaves.

Carina

I spend absolutely no time actually baking. Instead, I run deliveries all over town. Donuts to the sheriff's office and biscuits to the *Carmichael Lumberyard* every day.

Tobias is in charge of administration but yesterday when I swung by, I got to see him in action. All those muscles are not just for show. He was shirtless with sweat dripping down his chest as he swung an axe to split logs on top of a stump. Over the last week I've seen the equipment they used to cut down trees. But Tobias and his brothers cut firewood by hand. I stood there watching him split wood hypnotized by the movement of his body.

I wanted to lick the sweat off his abs. If Everett hadn't come out of the office to find me staring at his brother, I don't know how long I would have stayed mesmerized.

"Stalker alert!" he shouted.

I could have died right then. Tobias turned at his brother's shout and when he saw me, he grinned. My face was burning but I tried to play it off. Not that it stopped Everett from teasing me mercilessly the entire week after. As an only child I always wondered what having a sibling would be like. I wonder less now and I'm thankful for my peaceful childhood.

Despite Everett and Jonathan's teasing, Tobias never let me leave without a kiss. And most days, he finds excuses to swing by the bakery. The first time his mother caught us flirting I expected her to scold me, but she just smiled and carried on about her business without commenting.

When I'm not running deliveries around town, I'm behind the counter with Sam learning the register and meeting customers. So, I get to see how Everett comes into the bakery every morning on his way to the lumberyard to pick up a bear claw. But only if Sam made them. He turned his nose up at his mother's batch one morning when Sam was running late and left empty handed with a petulant frown.

The man has it bad, and Sam is oblivious.

"He'd never be interested in me like that," she denies. "We've been friends since we were kids."

"Hm," I hum in an effort not to push.

"Everett could have anyone," she adds.

"He could," I agree. The three Carmichael brothers are insanely handsome with strong jawlines and muscles dipped in sun kissed skin. "But he wants you. I promise you, that much is clear."

She doesn't seem convinced, but the man's affection is blatantly obvious. He gets mooncalf eyes whenever he looks at her.

"Well, Tobias is smitten with you," Sam says turning the conversation to safer waters for her. "He comes by just to see you."

Ignoring the burning evidence in my cheeks that she has struck a sensitive topic, I help a customer place a custom order for a cake celebrating her twelfth anniversary.

"You know you like him," she teases me as she restocks the cookies in the display.

"Of course," I reply. "But it's not serious."

"The man is literally coming by to see you every day and you think he's not serious about you."

Sam's words echo my own thoughts, but I refuse to allow myself to be swept away by fantasy. I've had relationships that started out hot and heavy only to fizzle out and leave me with a tender heart when the man moved on to the next woman.

A passing fancy.

I'm not going to let myself get carried away until I'm sure that Tobias is serious. We've sneaked dozens of kisses, and he seems sincere and open with his affection. I'm the one who keeps glancing over my shoulder to see if anyone is staring. No one pays us any mind and I wonder if that's because this is a casual and common occurrence for him. Just the thought of him flirting with another woman makes my blood run cold. Tobias and I haven't talked about the kissing or where this could lead.

Sugar Crossing needs a baker but that's not going to be me. Even if Elaine has the patience to teach me everything I need to learn ten times over I can't continue to take advantage of her like that. I would have already put in notice if I could find another job on the ridge. No one is hiring and if I quit this job then I'm going to have to move back to Denver and away from the man who is dominating all my thoughts.

It's selfish but I need to know if this relationship can hold water. If I need to find work in Bramble so that we'll only be an hour apart. Or if I need to run back to Denver with my tail tucked between my legs.

Can I even call it a relationship? We kiss. We flirt. We don't talk. We haven't gone on a single date. The trips to the lumberyard and his daily visits to the bakery don't count.

The bell above the door rings out as Tobias walks inside. For the past week he has always been the first customer. His grin loses some of its fierceness when he sees me, and I quickly force a smile I hope isn't too weak in comparison.

Sam murmurs an excuse as she dashes through the doors to the back. I couldn't repeat what she said if my life depended on it. He's wearing jeans tight enough to show the muscles of his thighs flexing as he walks and I'm trying to keep my jaw off the floor. No dates and only rushed encounters mean that I haven't gotten the chance to see more than his chest and arms.

The sleeves of his green flannel are rolled up to the elbows exposing his corded forearms, and I barely resist the urge to drool.

"We're rained out," Tobias says when he reaches the counter, his palms flattening on the surface and drawing my gaze to the prominent veins tracing the length of his arms. "No men or equipment to manage means I can finally take my best girl out for a date."

A quick glance out the glass display windows shows the rain falling in fat drops just past the striped awning over the front door.

"My shift ends at eleven."

"Perfect," he says before leaning across the counter to give me a soft kiss with enough heat to melt chocolate. "I'll meet you here."

Tobias

A week into dating Carina and I finally get to take her out on an official date. The early morning flirting at the bakery and the midmorning kisses at the lumberyard are great but I'm dying to get more time with my woman.

I planned to ask her out for dinner this Saturday since last weekend she worked the closing shift, but the rain came at a convenient time and moved my plans up.

Carina greets me with a warm smile when I breeze into *Sugar Crossing*.

"You are early." she says fixing me with a playful glare.

"Five minutes-" I start to say before my mother cuts me off with a snap of her towel as she bursts through the large black doors separating the prep and baking area from the storefront. Her timing is too good not to raise a red flag. I'm nine thousand percent sure she was spying on us.

"Go," she tells Carina. "Get out of here before the lunch rush hits and I chain you to the register."

My mother shoots me a look while Carina is grabbing her purse. It's equal parts warning and encouragement. Sam pops out of the back to wish us well and I don't waste any more time getting us out of the bakery. Locals are pouring in and while my mother was joking about making Carina work over, it is a very real threat that we'll get bogged down in small talk. Rain and snowstorms make the gossips extra chatty.

I don't fully relax until I have her squared away in my truck.

"Where are you taking me?" she asks once we've been on the road for a minute.

She hasn't been in Crescent Ridge long, but she has clearly realized we're not headed down to Bramble or to any of the local shops in town. Suddenly my plan seems presumptuous. I didn't talk about the details before I stole her away and it doesn't escape my mind that she might not be comfortable going back to my cabin.

"Uh," I start while searching for the right words. "I was thinking we could play some board games, and I could make some food."

"At your house."

"Yes." The word drags out into the silence. Only the rain hitting the windshield breaks up the tension I feel building in the cab.

"I'm really competitive," Carina says. She says the words with such a serious look I can't help but laugh. As I chuckle, she quickly adds affronted, "No really! Monopoly turns me into a monster."

"No," I reply with a grin stretching my face wide. "You're too sweet."

"Don't pout when I demolish your ego and force you into bankruptcy."

Our laughter fills the cab as I pull into the gravel drive in front of my cabin. If she's half as vicious as she claims I'm going to have the time of my life being thrashed by her.

"I do run a business, you know," I tell her as we walk up to the front porch.

"Not going to help you when I own half the board," she tells me as she toes off her shoes by the front door. They look ridiculously cute next to my boots. "I'm going to have so many hotels you're going to beg me for a loan just to pay your rent."

Unable to help myself any more I reach for her. She meets me halfway for a searing kiss that leaves me blindsided. In an instant her legs are wrapped around my waist and I'm palming her ass through the light wash denim of her jeans. White socked feet dig into the small of my back as I taste her until I have to pull away to breathe.

Carina's pupils are blown wide, the brown of her eyes darkening with lust as her cheeks turn a dusky pink that matches her lips.

"Not presumptuous?" I ask.

"A little," she replies. "But I'd much rather be here than at the coffee shop."

I nod my head.

"That *would* be a good idea for a normal first date."

"Normal is overrated," she whispers slightly brushing my lips with hers.

"So is Boardwalk."

Blood is rushing south and I'm losing my train of thought as Carina's warm body presses into mine. The soft curves of her breasts are pushing into my chest, and her thick thighs are squeezing my hips. I can't think straight. It takes all my brain power just to string along the smallest conversation.

"Hey!" she shouts as I walk into the living room and sit on the couch with her in my lap. "I resent that."

"Let me make it up to you."

Her breath catches and I see her eyes drop down to the hard line of my cock straining against the zipper of my jeans. I'm tired of hiding the effect she has on me and with no one around to see but her I don't feel the need to try. Let her see how much I want her. How I crave her body and soul.

"I might not be staying in Crescent Ridge," she blurts out.

The words are the equivalent of swimming in the river in the middle of winter. Icy chills slide down my spine and I swear my heart skips a beat.

"I mean," she adds when she sees the dark look on my face. "I still have an apartment in Denver and all my stuff is there."

"I can help you move," I offer.

Warmth floods back into my body as I slide my hands up her denim covered thighs, disappointed that the material keeps me from feeling the skin underneath that I just know is soft and supple.

"Tobias I can't bake."

This is *not* how I saw this date going.

"I can't either," I remind her.

Her little huff of exasperation hits my neck, and I fight my grin. She's so fucking cute when she's irritated.

"Your job doesn't require you to bake."

Ah.

"I'm keeping my apartment in Denver in case I don't find something else in Crescent Ridge."

I make enough money to support both of us. The thought comes unbidden. I can't say it out loud or she will run out of this cabin so fast she'd give a spring hare a run for its money. She values her independence.

"I could hire you to do the office work at the yard," I offer.

There's not much paperwork but it would be better than handing her a chainsaw and having her around men like Garrett Evans.

"No way," she says with a firm shake of her head. "I'm not working for my boyfriend."

She pauses, and I struggle not to grin over her labeling me as her boyfriend. It's the first time she's said it and I'm not going to make a big deal over it.

"I'll keep my ear out then," I tell her. "See if anyone is hiring."

"I could get a job down in Bramble."

Too far. My brain screams even as I acknowledge that Bramble is a hell of a lot closer than Denver.

"You could," I concede graciously.

I'd rather have her in the bakery or at the lumberyard, but I will take what I can get for now. It's too soon to ask her to move in with me but a blind man could see that's where this is headed. No other woman has slipped inside my brain and turned it to mush. No one else has set fire to my blood with the smallest smile.

"Or you could stay right here with me," I say unable to keep the idea of her moving in with me to myself any longer. Damn social conventions when it's right the timing ceases to matter.

"That's the plan."

For a second my heart stutters to a stop. Then I realize that she means in the general stay in Crescent Ridge way and not move in immediately and marry me way.

There is too much I want to say but I know if I blurt out how badly I want her to stay, how much I already need her, how much I miss her between our mornings and afternoon kisses then she will know I'm crazy. Too much too soon too fast.

And that's why I don't say anything at all. Instead, I grab her by the back of her head and pull her down for a kiss. I let all the emotion that's been building inside my chest since that first day shape the way I touch her. Let her feel the way I love her.

Soft kisses turn passionate, my lips leaving hers swollen as I drift down to her neck. She melts into my touch as I explore her body. At first over her clothes and then as she moans and grinds against me, I start sliding my hands along her bare skin. Layers of fabric find their way onto the floor as my hands and tongue map Carina's body.

"Tobias," she moans as I drag my tongue roughly over her nipple.

With her grinding against my cock, I take deep calming breaths to keep from coming in my pants. I'm dying to get inside her. To bury my cock deep and come inside her until she's round with my seed. But that's not how I'm going to convince her to stay. Until I know I have her love there will be no sex. This isn't about me.

"Carina," I growl. "On your back."

Quick as a bullet she's splayed out on the couch with her thighs spread open showing me her glistening pussy. She frowns at my jeans, but I make no move to unbutton them. Can't take a single step towards temptation or I risk giving in despite my intentions.

As I slide down the couch her eyes light up with surprise. She's grinning by the time her thighs are on my shoulders. Then with no more barriers between us I can finally dip my head to taste her.

My tongue cuts through her slit, sweetness bursting in my mouth as her grin melts. I listen to her gasps and moans as I take my time trying different movements. I circle her clit with the tip of my tongue before stroking it directly with the broad side.

Her thighs nearly clamp my ears, and I take the cue. She doesn't like teasing, rather she favors the direct approach, and I love that her moans become louder as I work her with my mouth. Always so quiet and reserved I can tell she's getting close.

Mindless to anything but the pleasure her thighs squeeze my head until I pry them apart. My cock presses against the stiff denim of my jeans and the cushion beneath my groin as Carina loses herself in ecstasy. With a white knuckled grip on her supple thighs, I don't let up as she begins to thrash. She trembles in my grip, her hips bucking against my chin, but I don't stop.

Sweet sugar pours into my mouth as she comes with a wail. I lick her through her orgasm and then the after-shocks not stopping until she is lax beneath my tongue. All traces of sugar wiped clean as I savor every drop.

"Give me a minute," she says. "One minute. Maybe ten. Then I'll be ready for more."

Patting her thigh, I place chaste kisses on the sensitive flesh before I stand up.

"Not today, Sugar."

Her brown eyes open in shock but I shake my head before she can argue.

"This was about you."

She looks ready to fight me, but I kiss her before she can form a protest. If she continued to insist, I don't think I would be strong enough to resist. As it is, until she's ready to accept all of me I'm going to be stroking my cock to the memory of her coming on my tongue every morning in the shower.

"Next time," she whispers before relenting.

I murmur a nonagreement, but she doesn't hear me. Her eyes are already closed, and she's drifted off into nap land. Just as well. If she saw the way my jeans are tented, she might have pushed the issue to my breaking point. Carina is a temptation like no other and I can only hope she falls for me hard and fast because I don't know how long I can hold off on making her mine.

Carina

The day after our date I try to come clean with Elaine. She's my boss but she is so sweet and with how fast I'm falling for her son I can't stand the idea of taking advantage of her kindness any longer.

Barely in the door, I skip putting on my apron. If she wants me to work my two weeks I will but considering how many disasters I've caused in her kitchen I think she'll let me go immediately.

I don't get that far though.

"Carina!" she shouts. "Tobias will be here any minute. He's going down to Bramble to pick up the new mixer and I'm sending you along. The last time he went alone to pick up my order he got the wrong equipment."

Elaine doesn't let me get a word in edgewise as she rants about the new mixer. Tobias shows up before I can insist on talking with her and he whisks me away without even letting me say goodbye.

"Sam will listen to her," he tells me. "She was like this about the new oven too."

The trip down to Bramble takes most of the morning. By the time I get back Elaine's excitement bubbles over and I've lost momentum. She's grinning as she lists the distinctive features to me, *again*.

"Four new speeds," she tells me. "FOUR!"

Sam and I share a laugh, and I decide today is not the day. Tomorrow will be fine. I don't want to take away from her happiness right now.

Except tomorrow doesn't work either. Elaine is heartbroken that Jonathan won't even consider letting her set him up with one of her friend's daughters. Or at least she pretends to be. I suspect she is trying to goad him into confessing his feelings for the woman who does the flour delivery. Her dramatic pouting and my own curiosity keep my mouth shut another day.

Then I have a day off and surely today is the day. Nope, Tobias takes me on a picnic date, and we spend the day playing and splashing each other in the creek at the top of the hiking trail. It's dark when we roll through town in his truck and find the bakery closed.

Each day I find another excuse not to quit. Elaine is too happy. Elaine is too sad. The bakery is too busy. And each day the kernel of guilt in my chest hardens a little more.

It takes a month for me to break down at work.

"I'm not a baker," I blurt.

Elaine doesn't look surprised at my outburst. She looks almost pleased. She abandons the cookie dough she was rolling out and turns a sharp-eyed stare my way. *This is the woman who raised three sons,* I think as I fight the urge to crumble and confess my sins to her.

"If not a baker, then what are you?" she asks.

Anything else would be the obvious answer. At this point I think I would be better use at the lumberyard. A chainsaw would be easier to use than the industrial mixer. Not that I want to be a baker or a lumberjack. I've never had ambitions career wise but there is one aspect of my future that has never wavered.

"I always wanted to be a mother," I reply.

"Then serve customers, run the register and give me a grandchild," Elaine suggests with no guile in her tone.

Over her shoulder I see the last person who should overhear this conversation. Tobias meets my eyes with his green eyes wide in shock and I feel the hot wash of shame color my cheeks.

He's going to think I'm trying to baby trap him. We still haven't had sex and he's going to think I'm some crazy lady who wants to trap him for life. I thought he wasn't pushing for more because he was serious about me, about us. Now I'm wondering if it was the opposite. If he didn't want to complicate our relationship with sex because he didn't see it leading anywhere permanent.

For the last month, his hands and mouth were all over me, but he hasn't let me return the favor. He always dodges my questions and my wandering hands leaving me with the impression that he's holding back.

And now he's heard us talking about grandchildren without him. At best he's my boyfriend. At worst I'm the cute girl he likes flirting with at his mother's bakery. I find myself praying that a sinkhole opens up and swallows me whole before I find out which. Never knowing would be better than this tense silence that sets my teeth on edge.

Tobias

"**M**other, you can't just tell her to give you a grandchild," I say.

My voice is stern, brooking no argument as my mother tries to run off the love of my life. My mother is unfazed, but Carina looks ready to cry. This is exactly why I didn't want my mother to meddle in my love life. It's barely been a month and she's trying to skip relationship steps one through five and jump straight to ten.

"Well, nagging you isn't working," my mother complains.

Unaware of the trouble she's causing she looks pleased as punch with her arms crossed over her apron wearing a smug grin.

"Can you give us a minute?" I ask.

I try to use my nice tone. The one I use with contractors and developers who buy our lumber, but she doesn't seem to appreciate it. Leaving with a huff she mumbles something under her breath, but I can't make out the words.

Turning all my attention to Carina, I fight back a curse at the unshed tears pooling in her eyes. Her shoulders are hunched inward, and I would do anything to have the confident and competitive woman who kicked my ass over a Monopoly board back. Not even knowing if I can undo the damage my mother unwittingly caused, I step forward until Carina has to tilt her chin up to look at me.

"It's fast," I tell her. "I know that, but I can't let you leave without knowing that you're taking my heart with you."

"Tobias-"

"Stay," I plead, grabbing her waist. "Please stay."

"I can't bake," she cries.

"You don't need to."

"But I need to have a job-" she starts to say, and I cut her off with a swift press of my lips to hers.

It's a fleeting kiss, a brief reminder of what we have together and what we will become in the future if she stays. With her trembling in my arms, I can no longer fight the urge to lay all my cards out on the table.

"Move in with me," I tell her. "I want to marry you, Carina."

"Tobias, I want to stay."

Not a yes but also not a no. I don't need her to accept my marriage proposal. Especially not when I've done the least romantic thing and just blurted the words out. Her eyes are still shining with tears and all I want is for her to stay.

"Then stay," I say. "You don't have to be a baker for me to love you."

"That's not-" she begins to say before stopping abruptly. "You love me?"

As if she even needs to ask. Her brown eyes stare at me in shock, her jaw dropped slightly leaving her mouth open a little. Five seconds ago, I was asking her to move in and marry me. That I love her shouldn't be the most shocking part of this conversation.

"Yes," I admit. "I love you like the flowers love the sun. Like you alone are the center of my entire world, and it doesn't matter that you just moved here. I'll do anything to keep you, Carina. I'd follow you anywhere if it meant you were mine."

"You can't leave," she argues.

"I have two brothers," I fire back. "One of them can run the yard. If not, my dad can step back in to help."

"Your whole family is here. I'm not going to take you away from them."

"Then I guess there's only one option," I say in a grave tone.

"I guess so," she replies.

The frown on Carina's face is upstaged by the twinkle in her eye. Her lips begin to tip up in a smile.

"You'll just have to stay."

"Really the only option," she murmurs in agreement.

I lean down as she stretches onto her toes, and we share a searing kiss. I don't even care that she didn't address the elephants in the room. We'll get there. With her feet planted firmly in Crescent Ridge we have time to hit all the other milestones.

"Elaine did say I could work the counter," she replies after she drops down onto her heels. "It would give Sam more time in the back, and she is a much better baker than I am."

I don't waste my breath agreeing. Sam has worked at the bakery for years and before that she was always popping into my mother's kitchen at home. Her and Everett would be playing video games up in his room, sadly not a euphemism, and she would come running the second she smelled my mother's baking.

"Tobias," Carina says.

My focus shifts from her swollen lips to her demure gaze. Every inch of me is hard for this woman and I feel like my skin is pulled tight as she peers up at me from beneath her dark eyelashes.

"I love you like bees love the flowers," she purrs into my chest. "Without you, life wouldn't be nearly as sweet."

"Carina…" I try to speak but my words trail off as raw emotion blocks my throat.

Reaching out I tug her towards my chest, burying my nose in her maple curls.

"I love you," she whispers into my chest.

"I love you, too."

The doors to the front of the store open with a bang, causing us to jump as my mother rushes over.

"Finally!" she shouts. "I was beginning to run out ideas of what to do with you. You are officially banned from the back. Do not touch any ingredients or the equipment. You are on counter duty for life!"

Carina's mouth drops open as my mother rants. Everything my mother had been holding back for the last month just comes roaring out.

"Five batches of cookies ruined in a single shift?" she asks. "Who ruins five batches? Carina, I love you. You are amazing. You will be a blessing as a daughter, but you are not a baker."

Carina's head tips back and she begins to laugh. My mother snaps her hand towel at us as she chases us out of the back.

"I expect you back tomorrow promptly at open," she tells Carina.

I wait until we're out of the bakery and my mother's hearing before I speak again.

"You don't have to work at the bakery," I tell her as I open my passenger door for her. "There are other jobs in Crescent Ridge. The tourist center is looking for a travel agent and you've got the experience."

Over the last month she told me about her year living on the road in a refurbished van. How she doesn't have many belongings because she was always spending her money on trips. Carina has seen most of the country by road trip and even went to Europe multiple times.

"I like the bakery," she replies.

"For now."

"What do you mean?" she asks. "Elaine is wonderful."

"She has nagged me to find a wife for five years," I explain. "Now all that energy is going to shift to you."

"It's not going to take me five years to give her grand-children," she says.

With her snuggled into my side as I drive us back to the cabin, I find my attention drifting from that distant future to one much closer. Carina loves me and I no longer need to hold anything back. She must realize it too because her hand drifts higher on my thigh, her nails dragging lightly on the denim. Her smirk grows as she notices the hard line of my cock straining against my zipper.

My breath rushes out in a whoosh when her hand squeezes me. The pressure of each finger grips me with confidence as I focus on the road ahead. I manage to make it halfway home before I can no longer drive safely. Pulling over in a small patch of dirt I throw the truck into park roughly before I turn on Carina.

Her giggles fill the cab as I pin her to the passenger side door.

"I don't have a condom," I tell her.

Never thought I would regret keeping them at home and not in the truck. We don't need to have sex right now. I just need to take the edge off and then I'll finish driving us home. Just the thought of Carina's mouth teasing me as she sucks my cock is almost enough to push me over the edge. So wrapped up in the fantasy I almost miss her next words.

"Don't need it," she whispers. "Not going to take me five years, remember?"

Carina

Tobias is on me in a flash. His lips catch on mine, his tongue thrusting into my mouth in a brutal claim.

"You going to let me take this pussy bare?" he asks.

Without waiting for my answer his lips go to the arch of my neck. Nibbles and licks twist my pleasure into tight knots.

"Let me breed you raw, right here?"

"Yes, to all," I moan as he tugs my shirt up.

The windows of his truck fog up quickly, obscuring us from potential passersby. This road doesn't get much traffic anyway. My bra lands on the floorboard and my back presses against the cold glass of the window. Tobias teases my nipples with flicks of his tongue before he sucks one into his mouth. White hot lightning races from the hard points straight to my pulsing clit. The wet heat of his mouth paired with the light press of his teeth are making my panties stick to my skin with slick arousal.

He lets me go with a pop, and I waste no time clawing at his clothes. I need his cock now. In the clumsy fumble to remove both our jeans we knock elbows, and I nearly send Tobias tumbling onto the gear shifter.

"Shimmy," he orders.

He peels my pants down my legs as I wiggle impatiently. Of all the days to wear tight jeans, this was the worst.

"Now you," I say reaching for his zipper.

"Can't wait that long," he says as he flicks open his belt buckle.

I barely get a chance to admire the long length of his cock as he pulls his jeans and boxers down his thighs before he's pressing the rounded head against my entrance.

"I've been dying to fuck this pussy," he breathes against my neck.

Wrapping my thighs around his hips I angle myself so he sinks deeper. Thicker than the fingers he's used this last month, his girth stretches me wide, giving me a wicked feeling of fullness.

"Live up to the fantasy?" I ask as he draws back before ramming home.

"Better," he says through gritted teeth. "So. Much. Better."

Each drag of his cock through my core pushes my pleasure higher, my arousal coating him as he moves. My head bangs against the glass after one forceful thrust and Tobias shifts us so that he's sitting in the middle of the bench seat letting me ride him. I keep my hands pressed to the roof of the cab so that I don't get carried away and hit my head again. Spreading my thighs wider, I impale myself on his cock, the different angle causing him to rub against the most delicious spot that has my toes curling as I bounce up and down on his lap.

"Carina," he moans against my lips. "I'm not going to last."

Me either. My clit is pulsing in time with my heartbeat. The sounds of our bodies meeting, the rough scrape of his jeans against my bare ass, every sensation is pulling me higher. Even the grip of his hands on my waist as he helps guide me is too much.

I fall apart first, my orgasm rushing through me as I throw my head back with a loud cry. My walls clamp down on his cock. His grip is fiendishly tight as he raises me to hover over his lap, the tip of his cock barely inside me. I moan at the loss before his hips begin to vigorously pump into me. His cock slamming into me like rapid fire.

My first orgasm rolls into the next as he holds me there. Unable to move, unable to do anything but take it. Take him.

"Fuck yes," he groans. "Take it. Take it just like that."

Aftershocks pulse through my core as he stills beneath me. Hot warmth splashes inside me and I moan at the contact. He eases me down, his cock sealing his seed inside me as we catch our breath.

Rain drops hit the windshield. Softly at first and then harder until the sound of them hitting the roof is almost like nature's own lullaby. Relaxing into his chest he strokes my back as I'm lulled into a peaceful nap. The steady drum of his heartbeat echoing in my own chest.

Epilogue

Carina

*O*ne Year Later

I never went after that travel agent position at the tourist center. Elaine was sincere about keeping me on to handle the shop while she spent more time in the back with Sam. Now I spend my days selling cookies and bread to smiling locals and tourists and running deliveries. I visit the *Carmichael Lumberyard* every morning just to drop off biscuits to my husband's crew. I can't deny that Elaine's plan worked like a charm, but there was a suspicion that lingered in the back of my mind.

"Why did you interview bakers if you already had Sam?" I asked her one morning.

"Over the years I've referred to the bakery and the lumberyard as family businesses and I'm afraid Sam took that to heart. Twice I tried to encourage her to step up to take over but each time she declined. I needed her to see that I was serious about handing the business off to a stranger so that she would get her butt into gear."

We roll racks of bread from the back to restock the shelves behind the counter. Sourdough, wheat, rye, and Italian loafs dominate the space but there are Challah, Brioche, and Ciabatta loafs as well.

"She'll be family once she marries Everett," I reply.

Elaine's grin stretches wide before she shushes me.

"I hope so," she replies. "But even if she doesn't end up with my son, she's still the only baker I would consider as my replacement. Almost thought I would have to leave it to her in my will."

"Dark!" I cry.

"Necessary!" she shouts back. "She's more stubborn than all my sons put together."

We laugh when Sam strolls in from her lunch break a moment later. She looks bewildered until Elaine explains that we were just talking about how she is finally ready to take over the bakery.

"*Sugar Crossing* needs me," Sam replies as she puts on her apron. "You were going to hand it over to someone who couldn't even handle ready to bake cookies!"

"I told you that in confidence!" I shout back.

Elaine laughs as Sam recounts the story. I cringe just at the memory of the charcoal disks. No salt or sugar mix up to blame this time, I just had to preheat the oven, stick the cookies in, and set the timer. I skipped the last step. Arguably the most crucial.

The rest of my day flies by and I close the shop in record time. I grab the cake I decorated today all on my own and my purse. The rumble of an engine cuts through the quiet shop just before a bright pair of headlights light up the inside of the bakery.

Tobias.

I have a truck of my own now, but I rarely drive myself to work. I'd much rather have the extra time with my husband. We were married a few short weeks after I moved into the cabin. My friends flew in despite just being here for Cassandra's wedding. We kept it small. Neither of us saw a need for a big lavish wedding. I wore a ballgown dress that made me feel like a princess and Elaine made our wedding cake. Sam does most of the cake decorating now but Elaine insisted that she would make the cakes for all three of her sons when they got married.

"Ready, Sugar?" Tobias asks when I rush out the front door to meet him.

He's surprised and he should be, it normally takes me longer to close but today I had a single-minded focus. To get Tobias home fast because I'm terrible at keeping secrets. Barely three hours I've known and already I'm bursting at the seams to share my news.

On the drive home I keep getting distracted and Tobias notices.

"Did you have another one of those asshole customers?" he asks as he parks in the gravel drive.

"What? No."

All the locals are pleasant and only the rare tourist is rude. Most people who travel to our little town for vacation are laidback looking for a break from the hustle and bustle of their lives.

"If you did, you can tell me," Tobias insists.

"I know," I agree.

"Then what's wrong?"

"Nothing."

"Maybe not wrong but something is off."

"No!" I shout. "I mean, kind of, but not really."

"Carina..."

It's not an ideal situation to reveal my surprise in the cab of his truck but he's not going to budge until I tell him. I gesture at the small cake box sitting on my lap.

"It's a surprise."

"Chocolate?" he asks hopefully.

"Yes, but that's not the surprise."

Unable to wait a second longer, even if I would have rather done the grand reveal in our home, I open the lid to show him the cake. It took some effort to sneak around Elaine and Sam to work on it during my breaks, but I managed. Tobias will be the first to know.

My breath catches as he reads the writing on the cake in the dim glow of the dome light above us.

Congratulations Daddy!

The icing is white with a baby bottle on one side of the eight-inch round cake and a rattle on the other. His Adam's apple bobs up and down as he swallows.

We've been trying for a baby from the start. Didn't even make it home the first time. I know he wants children. I just never realized his yearning to be a dad could match my desire to be a mom.

But it does.

I can see it in the way his eyes shine with unshed tears. In the nervous bob of his throat as he tries to speak, fails, clears his throat again, and finally gives up. The cake slides onto the dash and then I slide into his lap. He clutches me tightly to his chest, but I can still hear his shaky breath as he tries not to cry.

"I love you," he whispers against my hair. "More and more every day, Sugar. Sometimes I think I can't love you any more than I already do. My chest feels so close to bursting it's so full but then the sun rises on another day, and I do."

"I love you too."

Our lips meet in a tender kiss, the love we have for each other evident in every touch, every slide as we linger. He holds me there, rocking slightly side to side until my stomach growls. I'm tucked in his arms and on my way to the porch in a flash.

"I'm not fragile," I protest as he carries me inside our home. "And you left the cake."

"No, you're not," he agrees. "You're too precious to walk."

"Tobias!" I shout as he laughs.

He might find this funny, but I have no intention of putting up with this for the next seven months. It will get old fast.

"I joke," he says.

My frosty glare only makes him laugh more.

"I will do my best not to hover."

Even as he runs away from me as I chase him through the house, I know I'll endure his coddling. And there will be coddling, he can't fool me. It's going to be infuriating but I'll forgive him because I know his worrying comes from a place of love.

Crescent Ridge may have called me to the mountain but it's the love that Tobias and I share that will keep my feet planted firmly as we build our little family, and our love continues to grow.

The End

Check out Apple Pine to see more of the Carmichael family and to meet Suzanne, the moth obsessed autistic woman who drives Jonathan wild.

Apple Pine

Jacqueline Carmine

Suzanne

"Suzie!" Brandon, the newest employee at the Bramble bakery, yells when he sees me.

I've told him a dozen times not to shorten my name. I add one more to the mental tally before I grab the hand cart and start hauling dry goods through the back door. I've been courteous enough to remember his name is Brandon and not Branden.

"Right," he says with a sheepish grin. "I forgot."

Maybe I'll call him by the wrong name if he still doesn't remember next week. A part of me wonders if he truly forgot or if he is doing this on purpose. Is he flirting or is he trying to insult me? I don't know if I care either way. The nickname is annoying but only on a surface level.

Just when I think I've learned to interpret social cues correctly someone like Brandon through my understanding into a spiral. The autism diagnosis was meant to bring order to my life but instead it makes me question everything.

"Margaret said you're always quiet. I didn't really believe her until now," he mutters as he follows me into the supply room.

He doesn't offer help. Margaret's last assistant baker did, but he doesn't. It's fine, not like it's part of his job. But the way he leans on the hand cart resting his head on his crossed arms watching me work is a problem. I hate when people stare. I'm here to do my job, not to have some idiot waste my time.

"I'll have this unloaded soon," I tell him. "You don't need to supervise."

He jerks back like I've struck him. He leaves without a word and I'm just glad that he's not watching me work any longer. Margaret pops by with her clipboard a few minutes later and begins checking items off her delivery.

She doesn't make small talk or ask me needless questions. Her youngest nephew is autistic and I'm thankful for the space she gives me. Once everything is accounted for, she signs the receipt and wishes me a good day. I wish all my deliveries were like that.

An hour's drive into the Viridian Mountains and I arrive at my last stop for the day, *Sugar Crossing*. It's a small bakery compared to the one down in Bramble. Here I like everyone. Elaine Carmichael is the owner, Sam is her apprentice, and Carina is the server. And each one calls me Suzanne.

I barely make it inside before Elaine's three sons come bursting through the plastic doors that separate the baking area from the store front.

Tobias heads straight for Carina, his wife. She's got the oldest brother wrapped around her finger. More than once I've walked into the back to find them huddled together whispering. They keep it PG, but it always makes me feel awkward. As she comes around the corner, I notice her swollen belly and make a mental note to congratulate her later. Everett, the baby of the three, sidles up to Sam with a grin as he begins ranting about a video game they play together. He's the shortest brother but he still looms over the apprentice baker.

"You need to upgrade your armor," he says. "The Valkyrie mission is too high level for iron grade."

Sam cocks her hip as she frowns at the youngest Carmichael.

"It wouldn't be called a challenge if it weren't meant to be difficult. I'll make it through with the armor I have."

"Sam..." he pleads.

"No."

Even I can tell they're in love with each other, but they're oblivious to each other's feelings.

Jonathan, who was walking towards the back of the shop and thus me, jerks to an abrupt stop. He's taller than his brothers with a lean frame that never fails to draw my attention. His hazel eyes go wide as he stares. They shift from green to brown depending on the light. When they're green, the shade is an exact match for the *stinging rose moth* and the brown flecks mimic the *copper underwing's* pattern. I can never look away first, too distracted to realize we've passed some arbitrary time limit neurotypicals set for eye contact. When he ducks his head his faded blue baseball cap hides his eyes from me, and I find myself missing them.

I hate when people stare at me. But I don't mind when he does it. Something warm curls inside my chest every time I see him.

His mother comes bustling over, her round petite frame completely at odds with her lean string bean of a son. He bends down to kiss her rosy cheek, and I turn away. She's the only one who shortens their names and each of them have a different way of addressing her. Jonathan calls her mama and it's just the cutest thing ever.

This is my last stop for the day, and I need to get the van unloaded. Later when I'm finishing up the delivery, I see him eating a glazed donut. His cheek pokes out like a chipmunk from taking too large a bite and I stifle a giggle.

He's adorable.

It's a shame he's not interested in me. With my autism I'm constantly missing social cues, but I learned early on that if a man is interested, he'll let me know. Jonathan and I might share a moment here or there, but I've been delivering to this bakery since I took this job, and he's never asked me out.

Jonathan

Seeing Suzanne is like a punch to my gut. Her normal delivery days are Mondays and Thursdays. Not Wednesdays. I wasn't planning to see her until next week once the sting of her rejection had faded. It's too soon to see her after she turned me down.

"Everyone is going on picnics now that the weather is nice enough to hike. I'm burning through loaves of bread, and we almost ran out of flour, so Suzanne is doing an extra delivery every week through August," Mama says when I ask.

She notices my frown and calls me on it.

"You don't like her?" she asks.

This isn't something I want to discuss with my mother. It's not something I want to discuss with anyone, but my mother is too observant. Never could get away with anything as children. One time Tobias and I were shooting roman candles at each other in the backyard and my mother called home to let our babysitter know that her sons were misbehaving. She claims to have a sixth sense. Pretty sure the neighbor tattled, but the keen look in her eye has me squirming in my cowboy boots.

"The opposite," I admit.

Mama glances over at Suzanne, but the woman doesn't notice. The curvy blonde is too busy slinging fifty pounds sacks of flour in the open storeroom. When she's working it's best to stay out of her way. One time Everett tried to make small talk, and she didn't hear him until it was too late. In all fairness he shouldn't have been standing close enough to get hit with the sack of flour. He was covered in the white powder from head to toe and he stared at Suzanne with wide eyes as she scolded him for getting in her way. She didn't apologize and I fell for the woman then and there.

"Well," Mama says in a bored tone. "You are doing a swell job of communicating your interest. Avoiding her, not talking to her, and frowning at her are all *excellent* ways of getting a woman to date you."

Carina is close enough to hear my conversation with my mother. I watch horrified as she clamps a hand tipped with bright green nails across her mouth to smother her laughter.

Perfect.

Now she knows and that means Tobias will know in five minutes. I'm never going to live this down.

"I asked her out," I tell my mother, my voice low so as not to be overheard. "She turned me down."

"You asked her on a date?" she asks.

"Yes."

"Using the word 'date'? Or did you just ask her to hang-out sometime?" Mama asks the questions rapid fire.

"I asked her to get a drink."

"She doesn't drink alcohol," Mama says.

"I know," I groan. "So, I asked her to coffee, and she said no."

"She doesn't drink caffeinated drinks either."

"The coffee shop has tea," Carina chimes in.

We're drawing looks from Sam and Everett now and Tobias is back from his truck. This is beginning to feel like a family meeting. Or an interrogation. Same same.

"Ask again," Mama orders.

"No," I reply immediately.

I don't need to be rejected three times to get it through my head the woman isn't interested. I was clearly asking her on a date and if she didn't like either of the options I gave, she could have suggested a movie or dinner date. Instead, she said no and went along with her day.

"Be clear this time," Mama scolds as if I didn't refuse.

She acts like I'm not twenty-eight and perfectly capable of asking a woman on a date.

"Make sure you say it's a date. Be direct, Jonny."

My lips curl down. I don't need my mother's help in my dating life. She throws up her hands and walks away in a huff to help Carina restock the racks of bread at the front of the store. Tobias trails after his wife, leaving just Sam and Everett to witness a potential third rejection. But the pair are huddled over a fresh batch of chocolate chip cookies and seem oblivious to my presence. I wait until Suzanne is wheeling her hand truck back to her delivery van before I approach her.

Best to leave her the option for a quick getaway if this goes poorly.

Suzanne

I try not to stare at Jonathan as he approaches me. He's all long legs and confidence as he strolls towards me, and I eat it up. Chances are he just wants to say hello and be polite. Like their mother, all her sons are friendly.

"Suzanne."

"Jonathan," I say with a small nod.

For anyone else I would keep walking, and they could follow if they wanted to talk to me. For Jonathan I halt in my tracks. This is my last stop of the day and I'm ahead of schedule. Sweeping the van and clocking out before I drive home to an empty apartment can wait.

He takes off his hat briefly to comb his curly brown hair back with a rough hand before he slams it back in place.

"I wanted to ask you something," he says.

I wait for his question, but he stares at me expectantly. Waiting for permission I realize.

"You can ask me anything," I reply.

It's more than the simple 'okay' I meant to say. My voice sounds a little husky, and a different man would leap at my unintended flirtation. Jonathan doesn't bite though. His hazel eyes shine underneath the bright overhead light as he looks at me.

I'm missing context. He's still not asked the question. The one he went out of his way to ask me.

"You don't drink alcohol or coffee," he says.

Still not a question.

"Yes," I reply like he asked instead of telling me my own dislikes.

"The other day I asked if you wanted to get a drink and you refused twice," he adds.

"Well, I only drink water."

Alcohol just makes it harder for me to read people and coffee makes me anxious. I tried caffeine free soda, but I didn't like the bubbles. He rolls his shoulders, his tall frame straightening and I watch as his frown melts into a relaxed smile.

"Will you go on a date with me?" he asks.

A moment too long I stare at the perfect cupid's bow of his mouth wondering if I'm daydreaming. Or if I've hit my head and I'm now suffering from a hallucination.

"Y-Yes," I say. "I would like to go on a date with you."

His grin takes me by surprise, laugh lines crinkle on either side of his mouth as he adjusts his hat.

"Fabulous," he says.

A minute later we've exchanged phone numbers. He still has half a shift left at his family's lumberyard. I try not to smile too much as he says goodbye. I feel his eyes on me as I roll the hand cart back to the van and I try not to focus on the way I'm walking. Do I look natural? Am I swinging my hips too much? Am I walking too stiffly? My strides feel too long. The rattle of the cart on the pavement outside is too loud. The back door swings closed behind me in a loud slam that echoes through the parking lot, and I take a deep breath of that fresh mountain air. Summer is just beginning, and the scent of pine is in the air.

It fills my lungs, expanding them to max capacity before I breathe out a sigh. I'm this nervous and he just asked me out. How will I fair on the actual date?

The drive down to Bramble centers me. I hold onto that peaceful happiness until I get home, and my phone chimes with a notification. It could be an email. A text from a friend. Even a pop-up notification for this documentary channel I follow on Webflix. It's not though. Before checking my belly swoops with anticipation and I know it's him.

> I have a few options for our date

Options because I rejected him twice. Two times I thought he was just being friendly, but he was asking me out. That conversation replays in my head, and I feel a fresh wave of embarrassment coloring my cheeks.

I don't know why he asked again but I'm glad he did. Replying to his text I don't make it halfway through the living room before my phone chimes again. He replies fast.

> Dinner, Movie, Ice Cream

The first option isn't terrible. I don't love dining rooms, but it's expected on a date. I'm typing my agreement when he sends the second option and my heart soars.

> Museum, Takeout, Picnic at park

I can't type my reply fast enough. It's far easier to talk while walking around when I don't have to worry about fidgeting. And I'm less likely to maintain intense eye contact making him uncomfortable.

And the museum has a moth exhibit. I can finally see some of the rarer specimens in person instead of photos posted on the internet. Some of which are not good at all. But a blurry photo of a *smoky emperor moth* is still a photo, nonetheless.

I skip through the living room and rush to my closet. A museum date is casual, there is no need for an over-the-top cocktail dress for a fancy restaurant. No need to look up the menu online either. We can stop by a food truck or order a pizza for carryout.

Jonathan insists on picking me up from my apartment, and right on time at five he presses the buzzer.

I scamper down the carpeted stairwell like my leggings are on fire. My skater dress floats around my thighs as my shoes slap against the stairs as I huff and puff my way down from the fifth floor.

Bursting through the front door, I catch Jonathan by surprise. His eyes snag on the print of my dress and I feel the absurd urge to twirl. For such a niche interest I don't have many options but the *luna moths* fluttering across the black fabric do hold a soft place in my heart.

Jonathan is wearing khaki-colored slacks with a matching blazer and a blue button-down shirt underneath. His hat is gone and the way his curls tumble over his ears has me mesmerized. All I can hear is rushing water when those brilliant hazel eyes shimmer in the bright sunshine as he smiles at me.

"You look beautiful," he says.

"So do you," I reply before realizing what I said. "I mean handsome. You look incredibly handsome."

Now I've overdone it. Incredibly handsome. Mother have mercy. Could I make it any clearer that I'm dying of thirst and he's the coldest drink of water? Is that how that idiom goes? Or is it the tallest drink of water?

"Thank you," he replies with a grin. "Ready to see some antiquities?"

"No, but I am ready to see the moths."

He glances at my dress again as we walk over to his truck. Faded red with a loud rumbling engine, it stands out in the city of Bramble among the electric cars and sleek turbo diesels.

Jonathan lets me lead in the museum. He doesn't comment when I skip right past the local art installation. Nor does he complain when I breeze through the war sections. Yes sections. Four in total each with uniforms, guns, small videos playing clips of black and white footage, and a large interactive table filled with tiny figures to represent the armies and terrains.

No, he lets me go straight to the moths, following in my wake.

"So, moths?" he asks while I stare at one of three boards on display.

I nod mutely as I step closer. Each board has a dozen specimens delicately pinned in place. At the center of the first one is an *atlas moth*. I point to its wings as I begin to tell Jonathan about how it evolved coloration to mimic a snake's appearance.

He lets me talk, following me from one display to the next as I tell him everything I know about moths. Well maybe not everything, but I certainly give him more than a mere crash course in the subject. He listens intently, occasionally asking questions and unlike when I talk about my special interest with friends, he doesn't stare off into space bored out of his mind.

There are placards beneath each display with a chunk of text giving a brief overview of the three collections, but I cover that information and more in my lecture.

"This one looks like a skull," he says pointing. "So much cooler than a butterfly."

"Yes!" I say. "That's a *death's head hawkmoth*."

We're alone in the exhibit room. The museum didn't have a lot of foot traffic to begin with, but the small display hasn't had any other visitors since we arrived. And just like that I realize we're alone. I've been rambling for ages about moths while Jonathan has been by my side the entire time.

I love moths, absolutely obsessed with them. But there are a million things I'd rather be doing with the tall man at my side right now than sharing my love of lepidoptera. My eyes fixate on his mouth. The dark scruff of his beard shadows his jaw and outlines his lips.

All my moth factoids float out of my head as my brain turns fuzzy. Jonathan leans down until his lips are barely an inch away from touching mine. Waiting for me.

I don't hesitate to take his kiss. It's soft at first. His beard lightly brushes my cheeks and chin. Then his hands find my waist and my heels lift off the floor as I balance on my toes. He swallows my gasp, our kiss transforming from shy and gentle to fierce as he pulls my body flush against his.

The hard line of his cock presses into my belly, as a low heat begins to warm me from the inside out.

When all the air in my lungs is consumed, and my heart seems ready to burst he pulls away. I wasn't strong enough to end the kiss. Even now I want another. And another. I want all this man's kisses.

A throat clears and I realize why Jonathan pulled away. The intense blush that burns my cheeks doesn't compare to the heat still burning low in my belly. Grabbing Jonathan by the hand I lead him away from the mother pushing a baby in a stroller with another child clinging to her hand.

"Mommy," I hear the little girl say. "Was he trying to eat her face?"

Jonathan's booming laugh prevents me from hearing the mother's response. Since the museum was clearly geared towards my interest, I insist on him picking out our dinner.

"What foods do you not like?" he asks.

"I can find something on any menu."

"Suzanne," he says. "Food sensory issues go hand in hand with autism."

The low rumble of my name coming from his lips has my toes curling in my sneakers. That he responded well when I told him about my diagnosis is an added bonus. He doesn't make a big deal out of it, and I love that.

"I don't like spicy food. Or sushi. I like almost anything else."

"What about Chinese? We could call in an order and go to the bookstore while we wait." he suggests gesturing to a small restaurant. It's squished between two other upscale restaurants with outdoor dining but there is a steady line of people going in and out the front door. The restaurants on either side only have a few customers seated at their tables. Clearly a local favorite.

"Perfect," I say with a smile.

Jonathan buys the books I pick out, ignoring my protests. He insists that on this date it's his treat and my heart flutters like wings in response. In the end I get beef lo mein and Jonathan gets sweet and sour chicken. The food goes into a wicker basket he pulls from behind the bench seat of his truck. It's not a classic picnic basket and he tells me it's a family heirloom. An odd choice but I don't complain as we devour our egg rolls on the way to the park. Sitting next to Jonathan underneath a towering maple eating greasy noodles, I can't stop smiling. Not even when my cheeks hurt.

We share soft kisses as the sun begins to set. I don't have to guess Jonathan's interest. He holds my hand all the way back to his truck and even walks me to my apartment door before he kisses me goodnight.

Jonathan

On my lunch break I'm feeding Chonk the squirrel and sending Suzanne a picture of a moth I found on my walk this morning when Tobias strolls over. He doesn't comment on the squirrel. In the past he's tried to stop me, but he's long given up on that. I think marriage might have broken him just a bit.

Everett is hot on his heels, and I wonder briefly what has earned me a visit from both of them. We see each other at work every day for eight to twelve hours and our lunch hour is normally spent apart.

"So, you and Suzanne seem serious," Tobias says.

Everett tosses a sunflower seed to Chonk, and I'm momentarily distracted when he snatches it up and starts gnawing on the shell.

"Mom said you took her on a picnic with the basket," Everett adds.

"We're dating," I tell them. "Don't make her uncomfortable about it. We've only gone out a few times."

Three weeks in and I'm falling hard and fast. I took the Carmichael courting basket on that first date because it felt right. Naturally, my mother mentioned it to my brothers. I haven't been by the bakery since I borrowed the basket, and now it's obvious that my mother has sent my brothers to gather intel.

Suzanne likes spending time with me. She's always smiling and twirling in her dresses with her brilliant green eyes shining. Moths might be her hyper fixation but I'm the one drawn to her inner light. Like a moth to a flame.

My phone chimes with her response, and I smile at my phone to the sounds of Tobias and Everett's teasing.

> That's a polyphemus moth! Like the luna moth it doesn't eat and lives for about a week.

I realize too late that my younger brother is reading the text over my shoulder. It might be G rated. Hell, everything we've done so far might be PG-13 rated but that doesn't mean he can invade my privacy.

Swiping off the messaging app and onto the website I was browsing for Suzanne's birthday present, Everett guffaws when he sees the cloak I was looking at that has long wings down the back. It's designed to look like a *death's-head hawkmoth* and the reviews all praise the texture of the fabric and the accuracy of the design.

"You got it bad!" he shouts. "Looking at moths to impress a woman?"

The fact that he's right doesn't bother me. It's the way he flaps his arms to mimic a moth that awakens something primal in my soul. Everything is a joke to my little brother, but I'll be damned before he mocks Suzanne.

"Tell me Everett," I growl. "How long have you played that video game that Sam loves? How many years?"

I jump up from the log I'm sitting on to tower over my brother. He doesn't back down.

"You were so stupid. She stared at you every day with these huge mooncalf eyes," Everett snarls jabbing his finger into my chest.

My temper is rising, and I can see Tobias shaking his head behind Everett's back.

"At least I'm dating my woman. You are stuck so firmly in the friend zone you'll be man of honor at her wedding to another man."

He shoves me first and I nearly lose my balance. It's been ages since I fought one of my brothers and Everett has grown since then making the fight more evenly matched. We grapple trying to throw one another to the ground as Tobias watches with an exasperated expression. My phone lands in the dirt and Everett's T-shirt rips as we scuffle. We don't stop until Tobias yells.

"Knock. It. Off," he bites out.

I have a few inches on him now that we're grown but that sharp edge to his tone is enough to have us break apart. Both of us remember the way he would knock our heads together when we fought over the TV remote as children. And then to add to the insult he would take the remote and watch whatever he wanted.

Everett stomps off, but I know he'll be fine by the time we go back to work. We've had our share of fights over the years. We always bounce back in good humor once the ruffled feathers have settled.

"Can't wait for the wedding," Tobias says before he heads back.

Picking my phone out of the dirt I shoot Suzanne a quick reply. We have a date later today and I can't wait to see her again. Thinking back to how direct I had to be when asking her out on a date, I wonder if a straightforward conversation would help us move up our rating.

Suzanne

Jonathan arrives early for our date, but I was already on standby to buzz him inside. Tonight, we're staying at my apartment and making dinner together before watching one of my favorite movies.

He's been a gentleman on every single one of our dates. No wandering hands or anything steamier than a heated kiss when we're alone. I'm hoping that the privacy of my apartment will make him feel more comfortable moving our relationship along.

I greet him with a kiss at the door. My skirt and tank top allow more skin to show hopefully giving him a hint that I'm eager for his touch. The man is blind or oblivious. Our kiss is chaste and then he's toeing his cowboy boots off by the door and padding into my kitchen behind me on black socked feet.

"I wanted to talk to you," he says.

Ominous words but he seems relaxed and happy.

"What about?" I ask.

He kisses my cheek, the scruff of his beard brushing my skin before grabbing the chef's knife from the wooden block on the laminate counter.

"You like it when I'm direct," he says.

"Helps prevent confusion," I agree.

Over the last few weeks, I've opened up more about my autism and how often I feel left footed in social situations. In return he's tried to be more straightforward. He even weighed in on Brandon calling me by the wrong name. I start browning the ground beef in a skillet as I direct him into chopping an onion. Then he cuts mushrooms and minces garlic cloves, adding them to the skillet.

"Would you be open to expanding our physical relationship?"

My heart drops. I nearly lose the spatula I'm using to turn the meat as my mind races. Polyamory is certainly becoming more common, but I thought our relationship was perfect with just the two of us. I don't want to date anyone else. Not even just for casual intimacy. Maybe this is why he only kissed me. Maybe he needs more than I can give. But could I share him with another if it meant keeping him in my life?

No. I can't settle for less than all of him. I've already fallen too hard. My chest feels tight as I think about how painful it will be to walk away right now. Better now than five months down the road. Better now than after we have sex.

But damn it hurts.

"No," I say.

"Not ever?" he asks frowning.

"No," I repeat focusing on the food I'm cooking. "I can't share you with anyone else."

He pauses beside me. I can't look at him right now. Not when I feel like my chest is splitting open. Out of the corner of my eye I can see the stiff set of his shoulders as he stands frozen.

"No!" Jonathan shouts, making me jump. My eyes swing up to meet his even as tears blur my vision. "I didn't mean open our relationship to other people! We are exclusive. Monogamous."

"Oh," I say in a faint voice.

He raises his hat and rakes a frenzied hand through the brown curls underneath. With the food nearly done he looks at me with wide eyes, his chest rising and falling rapidly.

"I want to do more than kiss you," he says.

Those hazel eyes hold me captive as his words sink in. My little spiral was completely off base and judging by the twinkle in his eyes he knows it.

"I want more too."

Without looking I turn the stove off and move the skillet to a cold burner. Our lips meet in a hurried kiss. My palms slide against the soft cotton blend of his T-shirt as I rise onto my toes.

Kissing Jonathan brings me a sense of contentment that I rarely feel even on the best days. It's the caress of the softest fabrics, the texture of my favorite foods, and the boneless feeling of relaxation. His presence puts me at ease in a way I never expected.

And his hands finally wander. He pushes up my moss-colored tank top and slides his fingers under the waistband of my skirt. It's an overload to my senses in the best way. As he explores my body I return the favor. Under the hem of his shirt, I'm able to touch every inch of his muscular torso. The skin is warm and smooth under my palms as I rub them up his stomach and onto his chest.

Now that my hands are free to roam, I don't know why we didn't have this talk sooner. I could have been stroking this man's body for weeks. Like a match in a bonfire my entire body is set aflame from his touch.

"I'm going to taste you now," he says.

He spins as he uses his grip on my waist to lift me in the air. My legs wrap around his waist, my skirt bunching up on my thighs until the black lace of my panties is visible.

"Haven't you already?" I ask giggling.

"Not here," he says as he places his index finger on my bottom lip.

He applies enough pressure to pull it down and I open my mouth obediently. As I suck his finger into my mouth coating it with my saliva he carries me into the bedroom.

Jonathan sets me gently on the bed and I reluctantly release my hold on him. The green shirt he's wearing gets tossed on the floor, and I'm finally able to appreciate his body without it getting in my way. Acres of tan skin greet my eyes as I roam the plains of his stomach. Each delicious inch begging to be licked and nibbled.

He settles between my knees and as he flips up my skirt, I realize why he took the shirt off with a single hand. He pushes my panties to the side and a second later that same slick finger I licked slides between my folds. His touch is gentle as he explores.

Not pushing into my core rather mapping the area around my clit as he watches my reactions. The way I sigh when he drags his fingers through my slit. The heavy breath of my gasp when he touches my clit directly. Someone else might see the finish line and rush headfirst into ending the race. Jonathan dawdles, pushing my pleasure higher without taking the easy way. Underneath my tank top my nipples bead into hard points as he draws small circles around the bundle of nerves.

I clutch the sheets as my back arches. I want more. My muscles clench on emptiness as Jonathan continues to avoid where I need his touch the most. He toys with my clit. Circling it. Strumming it with slick fingers. Even once, a sharp pinch. All it does is wind my frustration higher.

Pleasure is there too but each time I get close he switches his technique. I could forgive a bumbling lover. Could instruct him on how to bring me pleasure until my toes curl and I beg for his cock.

He is anything but bumbling. Jonathan knows exactly what he's doing to me, playing my body like a maestro. He teases me to the point where I can't stand it any longer.

"Jonathan," I hiss.

"Yes," he replies, his tone warm and playful.

Those damn hazel eyes are peering over my stomach. I can see the way his cheeks lift. I know he's grinning.

"Stop teasing."

He doesn't reply. I watch as his head lowers until I can only see his brown curls peeking over my soft stomach. Somewhere between the kitchen and the bedroom he lost his hat. I can't miss it when his hair is so soft and silky between my fingers. The first touch of his tongue is electric. Softer than his finger and slippery wet it curls around my nub with ease. Caressing and flicking in equal measures he plays with it.

My molars grind until he slides up the length of my body. My hips cradle his waist as he leans down to kiss me softly.

"Are you finally done playing?" I ask him.

He grins down at me as his hand moves between us. I gasp when his first finger enters me. My back arches until my breasts are squished flat against his chest. Every curve pressed against unrelenting granite.

The second finger joins the first with a wet squelch. Soaked from his teasing I take his fingers easily. I squeeze my eyes shut and Jonathan freezes above me. His fingers stop all movement and I could cry from the loss.

"Look at me," he orders.

My eyes spring open and after a moment his fingers resume their rhythm. With my eyes locked on his, he curls his fingers. Warm heat rushes through me as he strokes my G-spot with well-deserved confidence.

"You're going to come on my fingers," he says. "And then you're going to come on my cock."

Gone is his playful teasing manner. He is focused, the movement of his fingers never wavering as I struggle to keep my eyes open. Eye contact has never been a problem for me. Something about the way our gazes lock makes my heart feel exposed. All the soft squishy parts of me are on display and the intense urge to look away is almost overwhelming. Only the fierce look of determination in his eyes gives me the strength to fall apart with such vulnerability. The green flecks are so dark they nearly disappear into the brown rings. My muscles clench around his fingers and ecstasy lights up every inch of my skin inside and out.

He doesn't move until the rhythmic pulsing of my core flutters to a stop. Then I watch with heavy lidded eyes as he pulls the fingers out with languid ease. Mesmerized, I watch as he sticks them in his mouth. Hazel eyes shutter as he savors the lingering taste of my arousal.

The hard line of his cock presses against my pussy as he leans over me. Still quivering from one orgasm I didn't think I would feel the beginnings of desire start to curl inside me like a warm caress. And yet I find myself arching to press more of my body against his.

The shrill beep of a phone cuts through the air startling us both. Jonathan's face turns a light pink as he shuffles backward off the bed.

"Let me just turn the volume off so that doesn't happen..."

His voice trails off and as he sits on the bed staring blankly at his phone screen I shuffle forward. He holds the phone so I can see the three numbers on the text screen.

911

"It's my mama, hang on."

He jumps up from the bed, jeans still unbuttoned revealing a tantalizing dusting of hair that I know leads straight to his cock. He paces the length of the room as he calls his mother back.

She doesn't answer. He calls his dad. No answer.

"I have to go," he says.

I hop up ready to get dressed and go with him, but he quickly shakes his head as he fixes his jeans and grabs his shirt off the ground.

"Stay here," he says. "I'll be back."

Jonathan

My clothes are wrinkled, the legs of my jeans stuffed into my boots because I was in a hurry. I dial my mama's number three times on my way to my parent's cabin. She doesn't pick up. Then I call the police. I tell them about the text message, and they assure me they're on their way.

Barely off the phone with emergency services I call Tobias and Everett but they're down in Denver picking up a table that Carina had custom ordered. They're at least three hours away, maybe more with traffic. I'm the closest to our parents and I can't get there fast enough.

Mama never texts. She always calls, insisting that text messaging is too cold and encourages distance. Every scenario running through my head just makes my chest tighter.

I beat the police to their house. Only my dad's truck and my mama's SUV are in the driveway when I pull up. Leaving the truck running I'm out the door in a flash. The tires are still rolling when my boots hit the dirt. My legs can't move fast enough as I run up the front porch steps.

The door is unlocked as always. Kitchen light on, table set for dinner, and the scent of my mother's chicken casserole cooking in the oven. No sign of my parents. I hear sounds coming from the back of the house where the bedrooms are located.

"Mama!" I shout as I run.

The loud thump of a body falling hits my ears and I burst through the door to my parent's room. Mama cowers under a sheet as my father begins to yell at me.

"Get out!" he shouts. "And close the damn door!"

They're fine. Relief fills my chest as I take my first relaxed breath. Then it hits me. My mama's bare shoulders. The blanket covering my father's waist. Their red faces.

I made it through my entire childhood without walking in on my parents having sex. And now, as an adult, that has changed.

I'm still standing shell shocked in my parent's living room when a sheriff deputy knocks on the door. By the time I've talked to the deputy my dad comes storming out of the bedroom in a robe.

"What were you thinking?" he asks.

"Mama texted me."

"Let me see that," he growls as he snatches my phone out of my hand.

His robe slips open, and I thank every higher power that he's wearing boxers.

"Lloyd?" Mama asks as she peeks around the door. "Is Jonny still here? I want to know if he used the basket. Ever is going to need it soon."

"He was just leaving," my dad says before he shoves my phone into my chest.

We don't say another word until I'm on the front porch.

"You did the right thing," he says. "But we're never talking about this after tonight."

"Agreed."

"I'm just glad it wasn't all three of you," he says with a self-deprecating laugh.

He sees the guilty look on my face, and he freezes.

"It's late and I need to make a couple of calls," I tell him as I run down the steps.

"Make sure you bring the basket by the bakery tomorrow!" he yells after me.

My trip back to Suzanne's goes by quicker than the drive over without my panic and stress making every inch of pavement feel like a mile. I try to call her cell, but she doesn't pick up. Probably in the shower. She buzzes me up and meets me at the door in a pair of grey sweats, her blonde hair still wet from the shower.

"Your mom, okay?" she asks as she lets me into her apartment.

"Yeah," I say with a groan as I toe off my boots. "It was a butt-dial with predictive text."

"Well, that's good news," she says leading me back into the kitchen where she begins reheating the spaghetti we were making.

There is something off with her tone. It lacks her usual warmth. I feel guilty for leaving her behind while I went to check on my parents, but I couldn't bring her into a potentially dangerous situation.

"Sorry for running out of here so fast. I was worried."

"It's okay."

Her back is to me as she stirs the marinara sauce with a wooden spoon. She adds oregano and thyme among other spices to the pan. Stepping behind her she doesn't react when I loop my arms around her waist. Nor does she say anything when I tug her back against my chest. I don't know what to say. What else can I say that I haven't already said? So, I do the only thing I can think of.

"Once I knew they were safe all I could think about was getting back to you."

I tell the truth. The words pour out of me like a river breaking free of a dam.

"Couldn't get back here fast enough," I add. "Even called you on the way back just so I could hear your voice."

I nuzzle her neck, smiling when my beard causes her to wiggle in my arms.

"We both know what this is," she says.

Her words stop me short. Pulling back, I wait for her to turn around and look at me before I speak again. I keep my hands on her waist as she turns. The warm heat bleeding through the thin fabric is not nearly as distracting as it was earlier. She's with me but her mind feels a million miles away.

"I know what this is," I tell her. "But what do you think we're doing?"

She stares at my shoulder, adamantly refusing to make eye contact.

"It doesn't have to be a big deal," she says with a shrug. "I've done casual before."

"We're not casual," I snap.

She flinches back and guilt colors my cheeks. I didn't mean to yell at her.

"We're anything but casual Suzanne."

.

Suzanne

M y eyes snap to Jonathan's. They swallow me whole, surrounding me until I can't do anything but acknowledge the truth I see shining there. The warm toasty mush in my heart is reflected in those hazel eyes.

He loves me.

"Jonathan..." I trail off.

He doesn't say anything. I can't look away. The hour he was gone was the worst. I was worried about his mom of course. She's always been kind to me even when I was standoffish and distant. When he left me behind, I felt less like a girlfriend and more like a hookup. It was a painful agony knowing that I was falling in love with the most wonderful man, and he had known all along that I wasn't the one for him. That I was just someone to have fun with for a bit.

Those dark thoughts swirled inside my head until they drowned out any reasonable logic. Jonathan has shown his sincere interest. Time and again he's made time and space for me in his life. He only left to check on his mom and he immediately came back to me. I might be miffed he left me behind but it's a small thing.

A soreness eased by his swift return.

"I feel silly," I confess.

The soft curl of his lips hints at a smile but there is no humor in it.

"You might have noticed I'm not the best with relationships. Or with communication."

The green flecks in his eyes shine brighter. The slight upwards curl of his lips grows until I can see a flash of white teeth.

"Maybe," he says.

I huff as I tear my eyes away from his. I'm vulnerable enough with my heart exposed I don't need to start crying.

"I love you," I say.

It's too soon but he needs to know. Needs to hear me say it because I expect he already knows. I'm always the last to recognize emotions, even my own. What I realized tonight has probably been smacking him in the face every day. My breath leaves my lungs in a painfully sharp moment as I step into the unknown.

"Love you too, Suzanne," he says.

His words are as soft as his smile and as warm as the caramel mint swirls in his eyes.

"I'm a mess."

"Yes, you are," he confirms. "But you are mine and I wouldn't have it any other way."

I slump forward into his chest and his arms slide up from my waist to hold me tight. His hand applies a gentle pressure that soothes the rough edges of my mind. Warm and soft, he smells like fresh cut pine, and I don't hold myself back from taking a long calming sniff at his collar.

His chest vibrates under my cheek and the deep rumble of laughter quickly follows the movement.

"Shush," I reprimand with a light swat. "You're mine. I get exclusive sniffing privileges any time I want."

"Hm," he murmurs. "I'm just a glorified candle to you."

"No," I reply.

My hands glide under his shirt mapping out the smoothness of his stomach and muscular chest. The green flecks in his eyes turn sharp with heat as my nails catch on his nipples.

"Wax melt?" he teases.

"No," I reply. "You have multiple purposes."

"Such as?"

I let my nails rake down his stomach. The soft hitch in his breath hints at how affected he is by my touch. How badly he craves it.

"A lady doesn't say," I tease back.

"You're not a lady," he growls as my fingers swiftly undo the button and zipper on his jeans.

I don't bother replying. The heavy weight of his cock is in my hand and I'm dying to taste it.

"Suza-" his words cut off as I take him in my mouth.

He never shortens my name. Ever since I told him I prefer it, he's always called me Suzanne. The abrupt shortening is just another tell of how affected he is. I try to relax my jaw as he hits the back of my throat. Soft skin stretches tight around a core of steel with no give as I swallow around his cock.

"I can't-" he starts to say but then cuts off. "We should go-"

Ignoring his pleading I work his length like a woman possessed. His stuttering breath and protests above me fall on deaf ears. He can come and he will. Eventually we will go to the bedroom but for now I'm going to stay on my knees and suck his cock until I feel forgiven for my foolishness. Until I watch him break apart.

His hands find their way into my hair, the blunt nails scratching my scalp as he grips my head. I know from the prickle of pain that he's gone. Normally so gentle and careful, his lack of control is telling. The tips of his fingers press into my skull as he unconsciously moves his hips, thrusting his cock deeper as he tosses his head back until the vein in his neck stands out.

"Su-" he wheezes.

I ignore the warning and swallow him deep as his salty seed bursts across my tongue. Drinking it down he rubs my scalp with tender fingers as he looks down at me with a soft expression. The muscles in his thighs tremble under my hands and I release his cock with an audible pop as I suck the last few drops from the head.

He helps me to my feet even as he pants to catch his breath. I can't bite back a smug smile when I see how red his cheeks are in the warm kitchen light.

"You look a little flushed," I say.

The glare he shoots my way is fierce as I cup his feverish skin with my hand and stroke his cheek in small circles with my thumb. His hazel eyes shutter and the tips of his dark eyelashes flutter against my thumb their touch light as a feather.

"Shush," he mumbles as he turns his head to nuzzle my palm.

"Maybe you should go lay down," I tease. "Maybe you'll perk back up after a nap."

His eyes open in a flash.

"Don't worry about me," he growls. "I'm ready whenever you need me."

Pressed together as we are I can feel his softening cock harden against my stomach. With wide eyes I glance down briefly wondering if I'm hallucinating. Refractory period who?

"Wanna know my secret?" Jonathan purrs into my ear.

I nod as I run a gentle hand down his length.

"I'm always hard when you're around. All it takes is thinking of you bent over at the bakery, picking up flour and sugar with your ass in the air."

My pulse pools low in my belly, my heart knocks against my ribs and I can't pull myself out of his hazel eyes. Not when he's looking at me like that. Like I'm the answer to all his prayers. The solution to all his problems. He looks at me like he sees me, and I know he does. He sees all of me and loves me.

"I like you best," I say in a soft tone. "When you're all hot and sweaty."

His eyebrow quirks and I fight off a fierce blush as I reveal a tiny secret.

"Last month you came into the bakery with sawdust all over your shirt and jeans. You lifted your shirt to wipe the sweat dripping down your face and I got the most delicious view of all your muscles glistening with exertion. I wanted to sink to my knees and lick your abs."

"You thought *that* was hot?" he asks bewildered. "I come home like that after every shift."

"Perfect," I say.

Heat flashes in his eyes and I know he's connecting the dots. I'll never get tired of seeing him fresh from the lumberyard, sweat and sap mixing to leave him smelling like a musky forest.

Dipping down in front of me he takes me by surprise when he hoists me over his shoulder and carries me into the bedroom. I bounce on the bed as he shucks his jeans and boxers down his thighs. My own clothes can't come off fast enough before he's on the bed with me.

"Come here," he growls pulling me down until I'm flat on my back.

"What are you-"

My question cuts off as his tongue slides through my slit and I realize exactly what he's doing. He doesn't pause or hesitate. Mimicking the movement of his fingers from earlier he brings me swiftly to the edge and I couldn't hold off my impending orgasm if I wanted to.

He laps at my center licking up the excess as my core pulses with aftershocks. I don't catch my breath before he shifts and begins crawling over my body. Each place my skin touches his feels like I'm touching heated steel.

"Still good?" he asks.

I nod, still out of breath, but he hesitates.

"I need your words Suzanne," he says. "I need to know that you want this as badly as I do."

"Yes. Yes, yes, yes," I chant.

Who says I'm bad at communication?

His hips bump into mine as he notches the head of his cock at my entrance. Slipping just a little way inside he pauses, checking to make sure I'm okay.

"I'm not a delicate little flower," I tell him. "Fuck me."

That first thrust sheathes him in his entirety. The feeling of stretching around his girth has me arching underneath him. It's more than the physical act. It's the soft look in his eyes that makes each movement strum a sensual chord within me. The wet slide of our bodies meeting creates obscene sounds that fill the room between our labored breaths.

His calloused palm grabs my thigh to push it up, spreading me wider so that his next thrust allows him to sink impossibly deeper. He feels so good I don't know how I'm ever going to let him leave this bed. Or why we waited so long.

"Suzanne," he growls. "You're so warm. So *wet.*"

I try to reply. I swear I do, but I can't find the words. They float just out of reach in the air leaving my head empty aside from the pleasure that's building into a crescendo.

Without speaking, I reach for Jonathan. My hands grab onto his shoulders pulling him down for a kiss, the tips of my nails biting into the sun kissed flesh. Even as the pace of his hips never falters, his tongue brushes against mine in a confident claim.

"All for me?" he asks when he pulls back. "You're drenched, Suzanne."

His words push me higher. The absolute filth he utters low for my ears alone has me dripping for the man, which naturally only makes him talk more.

"I never want to stop fucking you," he whispers. "You grip my cock so well. Squeeze it so tight, I never want to leave the warmth of your body."

His words rush together in my ears as I struggle to focus on both them and the pool of liquid heat he's stroking to flame with every thrust of his cock.

"Nothing has ever felt like this," he says. "You're soaking my cock, and I don't think I'm going to last. It feels too good."

My eyes roll back as my orgasm crests, Heat surges through my body as every muscle in my body clenches. My walls lock down around him milking his cock as I come. Every additional thrust feels like a livewire arcing inside my body. Electricity is pulsing through each nerve ending leaving me feeling raw and exposed. Everything is overly sensitive and overwhelming.

Jonathan's hips stutter to a stop as he comes inside me with a groan. His hot sticky seed mixes with the wet warmth of my arousal and I can't help but be proud of the mess we made. When it cools, I'm going to need a shower but for now it feels nice. He settles down beside me looping a lazy arm around my waist as we catch our breath.

"You're stuck with me," I say later.

"Wouldn't have it any other way," he whispers into my ear. "A wife's place is with her husband."

Jaw popping open I turn my head expecting to find him drowsy with pleasure only to see his hazel eyes peering at me with their depths clear and serious. His free arm sneaks beneath my pillow and he uses his hand to close my mouth before pressing a soft kiss to my lips.

"Marry me," he says.

My words catch in my throat, choking me as I stare at Jonathan with wide eyes. I watch as a wrinkle creases his forehead as he waits for my answer. The answer I want to give so badly if only my vocal cords would cooperate.

"Please, Suzanne. Don't make me beg," he pleads.

By mercy or by sheer will I find my voice.

"Yes," I breathe. "Of course I'll marry you."

The unrepentant grin that stretches across his face warms my heart even as he tugs me backwards into a tight hug.

Epilogue

Jonathan

S ix Months Later

"He's never going to ask her out, is he?" Suzanne asks.

I glance up from my cup of coffee to see her looking at where Sam is talking to Everett at the counter. The baker looks at him like he's hung the moon. Little does she know that he couldn't hang a picture frame straight to save his life. Even as we watch he leans nearly bending over the counter to get closer to her. They both have it bad.

"They've been like that for years," I reply. "Neither one has a clue."

"Shouldn't we tell them?" she asks.

"No," I reply with a grin. "They'll figure it out eventually. Wouldn't want to spoil the surprise."

"Jonathan!" she scolds.

We watch the pair as they flirt oblivious to the rest of the people in my mama's bakery.

Noting the agonizing look of longing on Everett's face, I concede that maybe my wife has a point. This song and dance have gone on long enough. I was strung out over Suzanne's perceived rejection for less than a month. Everett's been hooked on Sam for years. Someone needs to put the man out of his misery.

"Okay," I concede. "If they don't get their shit together in a month, I'll tell her."

"Why not tell him?" she asks. "He's your brother."

"I want him to feel as stupid as he made me feel about you."

Suzanne pauses with her latte an inch away from her lips. She considers my words before nodding.

"Fair."

Watching my wife take a sip of her coffee I eye the long column of her throat as she swallows. There is a small caramel drop of coffee left on her pink lips. Before she can lick it away, I dart forward and do it for her. Naturally, the kiss that follows is anything but short and sweet.

"Jonathan," she protests with a glazed look in her eye. "We're in public."

"We don't have to be."

We're waving our goodbyes and out the door a minute later. Coffee tastes better on the go anyway. Suzanne leads the way into our cabin, shedding layers of her clothing along the way. She moved in that same week when I proposed filling the empty space with warmth and light. Her shirt gets whipped over her head and lands on top of the *achemon sphinx moth* enclosure in the living room.

It doesn't have any inhabitants and won't for a while yet, but Suzanne was eager to set up the enclosure in preparation. Helping to raise endangered moths was always something she wanted to do and now she has the space. The Colorado Wildlife Federation will be sending her eggs soon, and she already has her permit from the USDA.

I trail behind her letting my coat hit the floor then my own flannel followed by an undershirt. I walk into the bedroom to find my wife lounging on the bed wearing nothing but my ring on her finger and a black silk ribbon tied around her chest in a bow.

It doesn't matter that we're nearly halfway through our first year of marriage. The honeymoon phase is still going strong. I crawl up the bed to settle between Suzanne's thighs.

"Always eager for me," I whisper.

Her thighs cradle my head as I dip down to taste my wife's pussy. Sweet like the apple turnovers she likes so much her arousal coats my tongue and I can't control the moan that rumbles through my chest. I don't rush to the finish line as I lick her. I take my time savoring every little hitch in her breath and each low moan that comes out of her mouth. Suzanne doesn't talk during sex like I do so each vocal slip is its own little victory.

I could jump straight to the tight circles she likes best around her clit without ever touching it but that would be no fun. Savoring the slow languid strokes through her slit I lap up each drop of nectar. It's not long before her thighs are flexing under my palms and beginning to tense with the urge to clamp around my head.

Pausing for a beat, Suzanne nearly growls when I don't immediately return. I huff a silent laugh before I lean back in to slip my tongue into her core. Thrusts mimicking the way my cock is going to pound into her I'm unsurprised when her fingers creep into my hair. Tangled among the strands her fingers give sharp tugs that guide my mouth back to her clit.

My grin is shameless as I begin drawing tight circles around the shiny pearl. No more than ten circles and she comes apart with a scream. Her thighs threaten to clench and squeeze my head, but I keep them pinned to the soft bedding. I lick her through her orgasm and only stop when she begins trying to wiggle away from my mouth.

"Too much," she murmurs.

Sliding up her body, she throws lax arms around my shoulders as I settle against her. Her breathing slows to match mine as I press soft kisses around the bow binding her breasts. She begins to squirm as I get closer to her nipples and it's the only sign I need to remove the ribbon. With a soft pull the black ribbon unspools leaving her completely bare to my eyes.

"Suzanne, you are a gift," I whisper before launching my attack.

She pants and whimpers as I suck, nibble, and lick her nipples. The small buds harden with my attention and Suzanne thrashes beneath me as I swap one breast for the other.

I pull back with a groan to get rid of my jeans and boxers. Her thighs fall open in welcome as I return to the cradle of her hips. With a single thrust I slam home every inch of my cock gripped by her silken heat. My head tilts back as I struggle not to come too soon. Suzanne's legs wrap around my back, her heels digging into my spine as she presses closer. She might be quiet during sex, but she never fails to let me know exactly what she craves.

The look in her eyes is feral as she silently orders me to move. Another day I might tease and torment her but not today. It's only been a day since the last time I was able to fuck my wife, but it's been a day too long. Yesterday feels like a lifetime ago. Teasing her would be torturous for me.

"Show me," I groan. "Show me how badly you want my cock."

Her hips arch to meet mine as I pull back before slamming back home. Her curves jiggle as I set a brutal pace. Each thrust forces her breasts to bounce and the movement catches my eye as the base of my spine begins to tingle.

Gaze rising, I see the soft glassy look of euphoria in Suzanne's eyes a second before her head tilts back and with a wordless cry she comes on my cock. Her muscles locking down on my cock making each withdrawal its own pleasurable agony. A second later I come with a moan as my seed coats her walls. Stars burst behind my eyes as her muscles continue to contract and relax, milking my length for every drop.

I catch myself from dropping onto Suzanne's prone form. Falling beside her, I roll onto my side before pulling her into a tight hug.

"Best present ever," I whisper into her ear.

Her soft giggle chimes in my ear as I wrap my body around hers. It's only been six months, but I can't imagine a life without this woman. The first quarter of my life feels meaningless in comparison.

As I fall asleep in bed beside my wife, I thank my lucky stars that I took another shot at asking Suzanne out that day in the bakery. And I conveniently ignore the fact that my mother gave me the necessary push. She likes to remind me every three to five business days anyway.

Maybe by the time we give her another grandchild she'll run out of steam. My hand slides down to cup the slight swell of Suzanne's stomach. In another month we'll announce our own addition to the family but for now it'll be our little secret.

The End

Check out Honey Oak to see Everett and Sam get over their fear of ruining their friendship for a small-town friends to lovers novella featuring dual virgins and of course the meddling matchmaking Carmichael matriarch.

Sam

My day starts before sunrise, bread doesn't bake it-self. *Sugar Crossing* opens with the sun and any customer who wanders inside is going to expect a muffin, cookie, or scone to start their morning. So, I get to work at three every morning to begin baking.

The mornings might start slow but by sunrise I'm talking to my favorite person in the world, Everett Carmichael. My childhood best friend who I've had a massive crush on since we were in high school. The youngest Carmichael brother always matched my nerdiness. We would spend entire days playing games until our fingers went numb or we ran out of snacks. *Legion I-X* we crushed. *Medieval Slayer* got slayed. We played co-op and single player alike. Somewhere between midnight server raids and code red mountain dew binges I fell in love with my best friend.

Then there were the times I ran biscuits and bagels up to the lumberyard for the crew. I still remember the morning I saw Everett chopping wood the old-fashioned way. No log splitter or chainsaw to be seen. He was bare chested, the same dirty blonde hair dusting his chest above abs that looked cut from granite. Sweat ran down his face, his sun kissed skin shiny as his biceps flexed.

I didn't know where to look. Every inch of the man looked indecent despite the worn jeans clinging to his hips. I tried my best to hide my reaction, but I know the other men saw it. My face burned fire engine red, and steam might as well have blown out of my ears.

Jonathan and Tobias made thinly veiled comments for an entire month after. To my embarrassment either Everett was oblivious to their teasing or completely uninterested.

If I thought for a second that he might feel the same I would tell him. But I've analyzed his every word for years. The nerdy lumberjack could *not* be less interested in me. Which is a damn shame because I love him and his family.

Running the bakery when Elaine Carmichael retires has always been a dream, one I thought foolish when I was younger. Now that it is becoming reality I'm thinking towards the rest of my future, and it looks bleak. I'll have my dream job but it's all I will have. One day Everett is going to send off for one of those mail order brides that all the men talk about. The sweetest woman is going to step off a plane and straight into his arms.

And I'm going to have to watch and pretend like I'm not dying inside. Someone else is going to join the family I love so dearly.

Elaine is like a second mother to me. She taught me all her secret family recipes between server raids and now she's slowly stepping back and trusting me with her bakery. The arthritis in her wrists is getting worse. She's allowing me to open by myself on colder days and it makes my chest tight. I hate that she's in pain but I'm proud that she trusts me to handle the shop that everyone considers another one of her children.

Tobias and Jonathan treat me like a little sister. They tease me for my obsession with video games and they mock my dating life. Or lack thereof. It's hard as hell to date anyone in a small town. Especially when your crush is never too far away.

"Still no boyfriend?" Tobias asks right on cue, his tone only slightly mocking.

"Can't you see him?" I ask in turn. "He's a little shy."

I gesture to the empty space beside me as I brush past the eldest Carmichael brother. Tobias laughs as his wife saunters up to me. Elaine hired her as a ruse to find Tobias a wife. To his chagrin and our amusement, her plan worked. Carina tried her hand at baking and then she was promptly promoted to customer service. Until I met the woman, I believed baking to be less a talent and more a skill. But no amount of training could prevent the disaster that was Elaine's first daughter-in-law.

"Did you hear about Julie?" she asks.

My mind scrambles but I draw a blank.

"Julie?" I ask.

"She's one of the Johnsons. She joined that SoulConnect app that Emma is always talking about, and she met someone!"

Ah. Another dating app success story. Watching as Everett talks to Jonathan, the middle Carmichael brother towering over him, I begin to wonder if I should put myself on one of the apps. He's never going to look at me the way I look at him.

"SoulConnect?"

Carina's brown eyes light up in surprise before she begins telling me about the app that helped Emma find her husband Andrew. With a town as small as Crescent Ridge all the locals know each other and besides Everett and myself they're the only gamers on the ridge. Plus, thanks to her chatty friends who visit every summer we know they met up for kinky no-strings attached sex.

Emma's told me a hundred times about the app, but I never paid much attention to the name because I've already found my soulmate. I'm just not his.

"Sam!" Everett calls out in his soft tenor voice.

Despite the downward turn of my thoughts, I still find myself perking up as he approaches me. The knowing smirk on Jonathan's face doesn't escape my notice. He's known about my crush for years. One time I was over at their house listening to Everett wax poetic about *Pirate's Retribution* and Jonathan took me aside to ask if I wanted to go to the carnival down in Bramble with him.

If I weren't hung up on Everett, I would have leapt at the chance to date his brother. Anyone would, Jonathan has always been handsome in a laidback understated manner. But I was obsessed with his brother, and Jonathan saw through my rejection with startling clarity for a hormonal teenager.

Ever since that day he's watched me pine over his brother with laughter in his hazel eyes. Jonathan's wife Suzanne strides into the bakery pushing a large hand truck loaded down with flour and other dry goods. He scurries after the curvy blonde with stars in his eyes. Like his brother he is completely enamored with his wife.

They follow their women around like ducklings chasing their mother on a good day but with Carina's condition, Tobias has hit a new level of obsession. While Carina is heavily pregnant and near the finish line, Suzanne's isn't inherently obvious yet. But we all suspect two Carmichael children will be born this year.

"Everett," I answer as my best friend joins me at the counter.

"Did you see that *Pirate's Lament* is getting a new DLC?" he asks. "This one is supposed to add a new storyline."

"Yes!" I shout. "And they're adding a new ship build! We're overdue for a tank to balance out the system."

As we chat about video games, I'm only too aware of Carina and Tobias eyeing us. The only person who seems oblivious to my fixation is the man himself.

Everett

I don't get much time to talk to Sam in the mornings. She's always rushing around the bakery at warp speed making sure that it opens on time. But today I barely get a chance to talk to her about the new DLC, one of our favorite games is releasing next month, before she runs to check on the cinnamon rolls.

My gaze snags on her curvy backside as she turns away. Like always my cock hardens forcing me to look away before I bend her over the counter and sink balls deep into the woman I've been in love with since we were teens. I've tried in vain for years to rein in my longing for my best friend. At times it seems impossible, but I'll do anything to keep from ruining what we have together. I would kill for the chance to escape the friendzone and win Sam's heart. If she gave me the slightest indication, she could ever feel the same, I would leap at the opportunity to show her what we could be.

"Sam is going to find herself one of those mail order romance agencies," I overhear Mom say to Tobias.

My spine stiffens and I struggle not to march over and demand answers.

"I thought she was going to take over *Sugar Crossing*?" Carina asks.

"Oh, she is," Mom replies. "She wouldn't be leaving. She'd bring a man here to Crescent Ridge to marry her."

"Are mail order grooms even a thing?" Tobias asks.

"Sure," Mom replies. "Sam's husband wouldn't be the first."

Just the thought of another man marrying Sam makes my blood run cold. My palms are clammy, and my chest is squeezed with a vice grip. Every sharp intake of air as I breathe hurts.

I'll be damned if Sam brings another man home. There is no way she would choose a relative stranger over the man she's known her entire life. The random man she meets could be a serial killer, or worse a lawyer. I watch as Sam comes out of the back with a tray full of iced cinnamon rolls.

"Dinner tonight?" I ask when she returns to the counter.

"Sure," she replies. "We need to tweak our gear for the new expansion."

I don't correct her. Our dinners have always centered around a pizza in a cardboard box and gaming. Tonight is going to be different. I'm not going to sit around and watch some city slicker move in on my woman.

Catching my mom's eye, I wait for Tobias and Carina to wander off. My brother acting like a mother hen to his pregnant wife, his overprotectiveness both thrilling and irritating her in equal measures. With Sam occupied loading up a display case I guide my mom towards the office in the back of the kitchen.

"What's the rush Ever?" she asks, bemused.

I don't mind the nickname. Only her and dad are allowed to shorten my name and Ever is better than Rhett. I wait for the door to close behind me before I speak. This is a conversation too important to be overheard.

"I need the basket," I tell her.

Her grey eyebrows shoot up as her hands land on her plump hips.

"Well, I never," she says. "About damn time you asked Sam out."

Not even bothering to question how she knows I plan to court Sam I listen as she talks about what a lucky year it's been. First Tobias, then Jonathan, and now me all meeting our soulmates and getting hitched. Personally, I think she's putting the cart before the horse. My brothers may be married but I haven't even kissed Sam, and Mom is already planning our wedding.

"She likes the red velvet with the cream cheese frosting best," she rambles on about our hypothetical wedding cake. "Although she might want something different for her wedding day of course."

Listening with a grin pinned on my face I can't help but imagine the wedding my mom describes. The sheer idea of Sam saying yes to being mine for all eternity sends delicious shivers dancing down my spine.

Sam was always meant to be mine. I was just too foolish to realize it.

Sam

Everett lingers at the bakery for longer than normal. He's usually the first brother out the door, but today he hangs back chatting with me about the new seafood restaurant that opened down in Bramble. Considering that Everett, like every other man on this mountain, has always been a steak kind of guy it strikes me as odd.

"Does it serve sushi?" I ask.

"I don't think so," he replies. "Just lobster and crab I think."

"Can hardly hold the title of seafood restaurant then. More like a crab shack."

His laugh sends a familiar thrill through me. With over two decades of friendship in the rearview mirror I've heard that same rumbling chuckle an untold number of times.

But each time I react the same way. My heart leaps to my throat and my heartbeat pulses down low.

Before he leaves, he darts forward pressing a quick chaste kiss to my cheek before waving goodbye without waiting for my response. A shaky hand rises to my cheek. Stunned, I stare at the clear glass door that swings closed behind him.

I can't help but memorize the soft warmth of his lips. He's never kissed me before. Certainly not on the mouth, but not my cheek or hand either.

This is weird.

It's only now that he left with Jonathan that I can fully focus on my work. Despite his distracting nature I can bake sourdough with my eyes closed but Challah requires my full attention.

Be ready at 6

The text from Everett comes through during my lunch break. Be ready? Is the man worried I won't have enough snacks? He's never left my apartment hungry. Or is there a new update I need to install before we login?

I make a note to swing by the grocery store and pick up some more of the salt and vinegar chips he likes.

Hopefully the lobster lives up to your high expectations

The second text freezes me in place. I replay our interaction this morning, searching for when our plan deviated from a night of gaming into a trip down to Bramble. With the hour drive both ways not to mention the time it would take us to eat, we would barely have time to reach the loading screen before my bedtime.

Tonight, we're not gaming.

I try not to get excited. The kiss on the cheek and then the invitation to dinner could mean nothing. We're so comfortable together that I'm probably building up what he considers a completely mundane interaction. He has two sisters-in-law now. Maybe he's becoming more comfortable with showing physical affection.

The trip down to Bramble is unusual but it's not outside the norm for us to go out for dinner. Normally we grace the little diner, *Lenny's*, that's older than my grandparents.

Still, I don't get many opportunities to dress up and by six I'm wearing a short cocktail dress. I bought it on sale a year ago but haven't had anywhere to wear it.

Tiny straps hold up a black dress with a tight bodice and a skirt that dances around my knees when I spin. It's definitely not something I should wear to dinner with a friend.

Just as I decide to change into something casual a knock on my door stops me in my tracks. Fighting the urge to blush I rush over to answer. It doesn't escape my notice that Everett didn't text me to come down and meet him like any other time we've gone to dinner.

He's dressed in black. The sleeves of his button down are rolled up to his elbows displaying thick corded forearms. The front of his shirt is partially unbuttoned letting me glimpse even more of his golden-brown skin. His hair is combed back and with the blonde and brown strands out of the way I find it impossible to look away from his clear green eyes. Bright and shiny like the sunlight reflecting off the blades of a fern after a heavy rainfall.

"You look gorgeous," he says. "I can't remember the last time I saw you in a dress."

"I should change," I reply already mentally debating which pair of jeans I should slip on.

"No!" he shouts waving his hands to stop me. "You look perfect."

His eyes dance down my body, lingering briefly on my bare legs. Goosebumps pop up all over my arms as heat pools low in my stomach. This doesn't feel like dinner with a friend. If I'm not mistaken, this is a date.

"Better than perfect, actually," he murmurs.

My heart beats softly in my chest. I always thought it would pound like an out-of-control jackhammer but it's feather light, like it's hesitant to believe this is happening.

Everett doesn't make a big deal about the heels I slip on or the tiny clutch purse I grab on my way out the door. The entire time he talks to me as we walk down my apartment steps. There's no time for awkwardness with him. Not when we're debating whether it would be better to play first as a paladin or as a rogue in the new MMORPG coming out in the fall.

I'm arguing rogue, it might not be the easiest role to start out with, but I think it will make the game more interesting. Everett wants to start out with the paladin who is featured in all the game play trailers we've seen so far.

"It's how the game is meant to be experienced," he says.

"A game is only as strong as it's weakest class," I argue.

There isn't a single moment of silence during the drive. Everett and I never run out of topics. The only time we've ever stopped talking was when the glue for his model airplane got into my hair. For an entire week I didn't even look at him. It was the most miserable week of my life, but he never put glue in my hair ever again. We told our parents it was an accident. In truth, it was retaliation for burning down his camp in *Legion VII.*

Despite the constant chatter, I'm distracted the entire ride down to Bramble and I'm more aware of my body than ever before.

We're at the height of summer and Everett has the AC blasting in the cab of his truck. Despite the thin fabric of my dress and the cold air blowing through the vents I'm still overheated. My body is on fire, and it seems like such an overreaction. Everett isn't even touching me. We're not flirting or teasing. But heat is building all the same. My panties begin to cling to my core, and I fight the urge to rub my thighs together to alleviate the ache of arousal.

"Hopefully it's good enough without the sushi," Everett says before we go into the restaurant named *Suzie's*. The building looks less like a commercial building and more like a home with red wooden siding and only a single sign proclaiming the name. His hand lands on my lower back as he opens the front door and ushers me inside. I'd melt into a puddle if it slid any lower.

"There's a revolving sushi bar on Bleaker Street," I reply trying to appear nonchalant and carefree like this entire dinner isn't sending me into a panicking whirlwind. "We'll just go there next time."

The words slip out before I think about the implication. If this is a date and it *feels* like a date, then I've already brazenly declared there will be a second.

Everett's soft chuckle follows me as we're seated in a cushioned leather booth.

"You ever think we'd end up here?" Everett asks after we order drinks.

"Not really," I reply. "Always saw you as more of a steak guy."

"Not *here*," he replies. "I mean us going on a date."

I'm tempted to skirt the question. It would be easy to play it off, and with a different man I would but not with Everett. He's seen me at my worst, and I know I can be vulnerable with him. Especially when his voice is low and soft betraying his own nerves as his fingers tap a rapid beat on the wooden table.

"I hoped we would," I confess.

My words shock him into silence. He's focused on me, and I find myself unable to look away. Not when those viridian eyes are locked on me with equal amounts of curiosity and heat.

"You never seemed interested in me. Not like *that*," he says.

"I was. I am." My head feels light enough to float away. The whole conversation feels surreal. This morning, I was making peace with his eventual marriage to another woman. Now we're sitting down to a romantic dinner and I'm baring my soul to the man who holds every fragile piece of my heart.

All my doubts disappear as I stare into his eyes. He looks at me like I'm the center of his world. All his focus, all his attention, centered on me. I hold my breath as he leans forward over the table. The very fiber of my being is wound tight like a spring.

The first touch of his lips to mine sends a shock through me. A second later our lips are sliding and melding like this is our thousandth kiss rather than the first. We only part when the server arrives with our drinks.

We don't talk about the kiss for the rest of dinner but the heat from it lingers as we chatter throughout the meal. Knowing that I'm not alone in this longing for more allows my desire to grow to new heights. I've kept myself in check for so long. Those years were filled with a desperate craving that only made my stomach twist whenever I fed that emotion with thoughts of Everett in my bed. I brought my body to a fever pitch imagining the man working my body like one of the machines he operates at the lumberyard. Sitting across from him as we ate our dinner was no easy task.

The tension pulling my core into tight knots lasts the entire ride home. It's not until later when I'm in bed alone that I can finally relieve that ache to thoughts of how the night could have ended differently if Everett were less of a gentleman. Or if I were bold enough to demand what I need.

Everett

L ife is different after that first date. Every day I swing by the bakery as usual to grab a bear claw. I know that Sam uses the same recipe as my mom, but I swear there is a difference between the two. It never fails that I recognize when Mom has baked a batch rather than my Sam.

Still there is a new level of anticipation when I enter the bakery. There's no unresolved longing or yearning. There is a budding attraction that is now permitted to run wild. I always kept myself in check through the years, never allowing my feelings to go beyond pure fantasy.

Now every shared glance is loaded.

"Don't worry," Carina teases as I walk up to the counter. "Sam made this batch."

She hands over the bear claw before calling Sam to the front.

"Your boyfriend is here," she says.

It shouldn't affect me so strongly, but I find myself standing straighter with a pep in my step. My brothers and sisters-in-law have always made jokes but now the label is fitting. Sam is my girlfriend.

"You're going to get fat," the woman of the hour says when she sees me.

"Unlikely," I reply. "But I'll make sure I chop some wood the old-fashioned way to burn the extra calories."

Her face turns a delicious shade of pink even before I wink. Pieces click together at an alarming rate.

"Jonathan's teasing wasn't unfounded," I mumble.

My brother doesn't have a knack for subtlety. It's clear that he's been dropping hints for a while. She doesn't meet my gaze, her blush darkening to a bold red under my scrutiny.

"No," she says.

"All of it?" I ask.

Sam bites her lips before glancing over her shoulder at the black doors that lead to the kitchen. It's so early in the morning that we're alone in the bakery aside from my family but they're all gathered in the back.

Her nod, as silent as it is, might as well be the boom of a cannon shot. Memories flood my brain, years of my older brothers calling Sam my wife and teasing us for acting like an old married couple.

One day when Sam brought us breakfast to the lumber-yard, I was chopping wood with an axe. It's not something that is necessary with the logging equipment we have but every so often it feels good to work out some aggression with physical exertion. I can't remember why I was pissed that day but I'm sure it was something Jonathan did.

He's always playing pranks and making dumb comments. Just like he did when Sam saw me with the axe. It was warm for a spring morning, and I thought her face was red from the unexpected heat. I could smack myself in the face as every single one of my brother's jokes comes roaring back into my brain.

"Lovebirds," he called us one time when he saw us sitting on a bench together at the park.

"Are you going to ever going to buy the cow or just keep looking at it?" I overheard him ask Sam a different day.

"Trade the video games for bingo and y'all are already in your sunset years," Jonathan said once when he caught us in a zombie state after the midnight release of *Legion VIII*.

We pulled an all-nighter to play the game, and my brothers had no shortage of jokes about what they would do if they had a girl in their room all night. I was a teenage boy, and I had all the same thoughts. I would have trashed *Legion VIII* in a heartbeat if Sam seemed interested in me.

Apparently, she had, and I was the only idiot not to notice.

"We fucked up," I say, still shell shocked from her revelation.

"Excuse me?"

"Years, Sam. Years."

She rolls her eyes at me with a huff, but a glimmer of regret shines in her blue eyes. Like me I'm sure she's replaying memories, wondering how our lives would be different if either of us had confessed our feelings sooner. We would be high school sweethearts with three kids by now.

Then the distinct memory of what a dumbass I was in my teenage years hits and I become thankful she didn't see *all* of it.

I ask her to dinner, because what else should I do when the woman I love is finally mine. We might have missed out on some good memories, probably some messy ones too, but we've got all the time in the world to make better ones.

The future is looking good.

Sam

I'm on cloud freaking nine all day. Carina shoots more than one suspicious look my way and I know it's because of the grin on my face. It doesn't matter what happens, I can't stop smiling. Not even when I'm doing paperwork in the back. Suzanne, Jonathan's wife and our supplier, notices too. She starts to say something, and I cut her off with a quick question about inventory. Then I make my excuses to go cover the front for Carina's break.

Everett isn't making a big deal about our relationship yet. Aside from the kiss, nothing has really changed. We still talk about games, and work. We still joke and laugh, the same as always. I'm sure from the outside everything is the exact way it's always been. But now there is a delicious undercurrent of tension with every interaction. With our mutual attraction out in the open, there's no more hiding behind covert glances. We can look our fill.

"Sugar," Tobias calls as he enters the shop.

His green eyes meet mine and awkward silence begins to float around us. He didn't look before he attempted to greet Carina and for once it was not his wife behind the counter.

"She's in the back," I say pointing a finger over my shoulder. "On break."

He looks relieved that I've taken mercy on him, the furrow of his brow smoothing out as the tension bleeds from his stance. As he goes to the back he pauses to ask, "You won't mention this right?"

If I humored the idea of teasing him for the faux paus, it's dashed by the thought of Carina. She's nearing the end of her pregnancy and emotions are running high. Earlier she nearly cried because she couldn't see her feet. I'm not going to risk adding anything to the teetering tower of her psyche right now.

"Lips are sealed."

Everett breezes into the bakery a second after Tobias steps into the back. With Jonathan already outside, helping Suzanne unload our latest delivery from her van, he's the last to arrive.

"Hey there handsome," I say with a cheerful smile that makes my cheeks hurt.

"Sam," he greets me in turn. "Please tell me the bear claws are yours."

I try not to wince at his flat tone. His hair is still messy from sleep with one side flattened from where he laid on his pillow. Everett has never been a morning person.

"Why do you like them so much?" I ask, genuinely curious.

The man has come in every morning to get a bear claw since I started working here. I can't remember a day when he skipped the indulgence.

"Cause you make them," he mumbles around a mouthful of pastry.

His words bring me up short. Grumpy demeanor aside, his words hold promise and a hint of vulnerability. He might not flaunt his affection but it's there.

"I make more than bear claws you know," I joke for lack of anything else to say in reply.

"Yeah," he says between bites. "But these are the best."

He hangs around for a few more minutes making small talk before he heads to work. Tobias and Jonathan follow a few minutes later. Despite the way they linger saying goodbyes to their wives they'll still be at the lumberyard before any of the crew. It might be a family business, but their dad taught them to lead by example. They're the first ones on site and the last to leave every day.

It's a busy day but I can't help but hope that I'll see Everett again. Tobias swings by to visit Carina on his lunch break and I don't have the courage to ask if his brother is headed down the mountain too. Each time I bring racks of bread fresh from the oven I check the front with hopeful apprehension. By the end of day, the shelves out front are full, and we'll be selling the overstock at half price tomorrow. Seeing the physical proof of my overbaking I can't help but accept that I'm bothered by Everett's lack of public affection.

Carina lingers by the counter when we close, sending Tobias back out to their truck with her purse and a box of pastries.

"Spill," she says tapping her purple coffin nail against the counter.

I glance at the front door, not wanting Tobias to overhear and she rolls her brown eyes.

"The cinnamon rolls will keep him busy," she says. "Now tell me what's going on. I've been here over a year, and I've never seen you bake so much extra."

Looking at the full shelves behind us I can't help but wince. If Elaine saw this, she would be furious. I wouldn't blame her. This is a novice mistake.

"I was a bit distracted."

Carina crosses her arms with an unimpressed look. She looks almost comical as she tries to scowl at me.

"A bit?" she asks skeptically. "You over baked every single kind of bread we sell. Even the pumpernickel! We mark that down every day and yet you still made an extra three dozen."

Something inside me breaks and I find myself telling her exactly what she wants to know.

"Everett and I are-" I begin but she interrupts me with a squeal as she bounces up and down on her toes.

"Finally!" she shouts.

"You can't tell anyone!" I shout back, glancing towards the front door.

Tobias might be busy for now, but he can eat a pastry per minute. I know because the brothers used to race and time themselves. Tobias is the fastest with Everett being a close second. Jonathan never got the hang of it, instead of swallowing he would stuff his face till his cheeks puffed out like a chipmunk. Elaine used to call him her little chipmunk when he was younger. All it took for that to stop was a high school girlfriend hearing it and an unsettling amount of tears. Now she just sticks to shortening their names. Toby, Jonny, and Ever.

"Pinky promise," she says holding out her hand with her pinky extended to shake mine. I take the offer, as I struggle to find the right words.

"I think he's ashamed of me," I confess.

Carina starts shaking her head before I finish.

"No. No way. I've been telling you since the beginning that the man is in love with you."

"I don't doubt his feelings."

"Just whether he's serious about your relationship."

"Precisely."

Carina tries her best to reassure me before Tobias eventually comes back to find out why his wife is lingering. She leaves with a mild look of regret, and I wave goodbye. There is nothing she can say that will bandage my wounded pride. Despite her assertive stance that Everett is serious about me I can't help but have my doubts.

Everett

All three of us own the lumberyard jointly but Tobias has always taken the lead. He does all the paperwork while Jonathan handles daily management. With barely any extra responsibility on my shoulders I volunteer to supervise overtime when it's needed so my brothers can get back to their families sooner. With both Carina and Suzanne pregnant I expect that I'll be working longer hours for the next year or so. But I know when the time comes for Sam and me, they'll do the same for us.

With a large shipment due out by the weekend I skipped my lunch break to get caught up on some routine maintenance. Later when I call Sam after I finally wrap up the workday and send the last of the crew home she doesn't answer. Buzz, the oldest member of our crew, smirks when he sees me redialing her number again. *Sugar Crossing* closed hours ago and I know that Sam should be at home in her apartment by now.

"Hoo boy! Someone's in hot water!" he shouts as he heads to his truck. Before his laughter fades away, I'm sent to voicemail again.

Today was a long one. Call me

I keep it short figuring I'll tell her more about it when we talk later. I'd love to have dinner with her, but I doubt she wants me to show up unannounced to her apartment especially when I'm covered in sweat and sawdust.

My cabin isn't far from the lumberyard. I go out of my way each morning to visit Sam at the bakery but it's worth seeing her smiling face. Not to mention the hit of sugar from her bear claws.

It's a short drive home and then I'm finally able to shower. The hot water works miracles on my sore muscles. After I can barely do more than shuffle my feet towards the kitchen. I've never been much of a baker, neither are my brothers, but I can cook with the best of them. With my mom always working around ovens she never wanted to cook at home and that is where my dad has always shined. My dad cooked every meal unless he was sick. It didn't matter how many hours he worked at the lumberyard he never let my mother do more than turn on the slow cooker.

It's been a long day and with just myself to feed I don't need to do anything super fancy. A basic omelet with peppers, onions, and cheese will do. The peppers and onions are already sliced, and past me is getting a lot of brownie points for that decision. The hot food goes further to soothe my aching body, and I debate calling Sam again. There's hardly been a day we haven't spoken to each other. It feels off, but I don't want to bother her. She wakes up early to open the bakery.

Lying in my bed I stare at my phone screen, tempted to call her just for the hell of it. But she might already be asleep, and I don't want to wake her.

This is my first time having a girlfriend and my lack of experience is evident. No one ever could measure up to Sam. None of the girls who have tried to flirt with me could ever compare to my best friend. I didn't date in high school, or after. I don't think Sam has either. This is uncharted territory for both of us.

Ultimately, I decide not to call her even though I can't help but feel that something is off. It's not like Sam to ignore my messages. Even if she didn't want to talk, she would still send a text. I can't help but worry that I've missed a step and fucked up.

Sam

All night I tossed and turned, unable to make peace with the gnawing pit in my stomach. I even turned off my phone after work because I didn't want to give into the temptation to call Everett. We've been friends forever and no matter what I don't want to lose that bond. I didn't want to reach out in a low moment with my emotions running rampant and ruin our friendship.

Elaine knows something is up the second she enters the bakery. I don't know if it's something I'm doing unconsciously or the look on my face. She looks at me like she can see right through me to all the raw vulnerable bits. It reminds me of the way my own mother looks at me when I visit. She sees more than what's on the surface.

I don't give her a chance to ask though.

"I heard Daniel and Lily are expecting again," I say the second there is a lull in the conversation.

It does a decent job of distracting her as we chat about the Hart family and their rambunctious children. Lily was the first mail order bride to move to Crescent Ridge several years ago. Her sister followed soon after, marrying another of the men who call this mountain home and then it seemed like every month there was a new bride on her way to our small town.

Most of the town's firefighters have sent for brides and with Everett and his brothers working as volunteers to fight wildfires I was always worried he would eventually succumb to the temptation.

By the time Carina comes in to open the front I've managed to keep the conversation on safe topics. With Tobias and his wife within earshot, Elaine's curiosity is hogtied for the moment.

"I'm not going to break!" Carina shouts at her husband.

Elaine is drawn to her distressed daughter-in-law's plight like a moth to flame.

"Tell him he's a fool!" Carina cries to Elaine. "The man is talking about bed rest. I do not need bed rest. I swear if he locks me up in that cabin-"

I duck away as Tobias flutters around his wife trying to cool her ire.

"Would never go that far," he mutters. "This much stress isn't good for the baby-"

"I wouldn't be stressed if you could keep your neanderthal opinions to yourself!" Carina fires back before I escape to the front of the store.

There isn't much to do behind the counter, but I have zero intention of hanging around to witness Tobias' miscommunication mix with his wife's pregnancy hormones. Elaine is there to mediate. She can handle it.

Setting up the tables only takes a minute but before I've finished the bell over the door rings out. I turn to find Everett standing just inside the doorway. It's a workday but he's not wearing his usual worn jeans and flannel combo. He's wearing a bright blue button down and khaki pants that cling to the sculpted curves of his thighs.

"Good morning, Sam," he says. The unmistakable Carmichael courting basket dangles from his hand. "The bakery is going to have to manage without you for the day."

He looks good in the early morning light. That unruly blonde hair of his is combed and I'm tempted to run my fingers through the strands until it's a mess again. As gorgeous as he is, my eyes keep straying to the basket clutched tightly in his hand.

"I would have picked you up from your home, but I thought a few pastries would go perfectly with the lunch I made," he says. "Plus, I thought it was well overdue to declare my intentions."

"Shut up," I snap with embarrassment rather than anger coloring my tone.

Everett's responding grin mirrors the bubble of happiness blooming in my chest.

"Who am I but a lowly lumberjack-"

"Stop," I cry dashing over to close the distance between us. "You really brought the basket."

"Of course," he replies. "I asked for it the same day we went to dinner."

My hand slams into his chest with more force than is polite. Everett winces as he lays his free hand over mine, pressing my palm against his chest.

"I didn't want to ruin this by rushing," he says.

The vulnerable look in his soft green eyes soothes the chafed pieces of my heart.

"Neither did I," I confess.

He sets the basket on the table closest to us.

"I don't want to do anything with you by half measures," he says as he sinks down onto one knee. "I have loved you as long as I have known you. Somewhere that love became less than platonic. It didn't happen all at once but one day I realized that my feelings had changed. My love was no longer the wholesome love of a friend but something deeper and darker. Something with sharp edges and tender flesh. I knew I wouldn't be able to handle your rejection, so I hid behind our friendship like a coward. I'm not hiding anymore."

The sight of Everett on one knee sends butterflies dancing through my chest. My heart beats quick and light as I try not to cry.

"Will you marry me?" he asks.

A sob chokes me as warm tears run down my face. It's difficult to speak with happiness and relief clawing at my throat. My free hand goes to my throat even as Everett keeps my other in a soft grip as he looks up at me earnestly. I haven't answered the man.

Why haven't I answered him?

"Y-Yes," I stutter. "Of course I'll marry you. I've loved you for years. I thought you didn't want anything serious."

"That's why you didn't call me last night," Everett says as he stands up.

"In a roundabout way," I murmur. "It's been turned off since yesterday because I didn't want to bother you."

"You could never bother me," he says.

I can't help but laugh.

"Remember this moment when you are tempted to call me a nagging wife in ten years."

He doesn't deny it. Just presses close and kisses me like it's the last kiss we'll ever have. There's warmth and urgency but at once it's soft and languid. He kisses me like he's savoring the experience.

One day the sweetness from this day will temper from a bright burst into a smooth richness. Our love will only grow deeper with time.

Clapping makes us jump apart. I spin around to find Elaine, her sons, and their wives all cheering for us. The only Carmichael missing is the father, Lloyd. He'll be madder than a wet hen that he missed his youngest son's proposal.

"Congratulations," Tobias and Carina chime together.

Their fight is old news with Tobias seeming just slightly on edge as he tries to support his wife without crowding her.

"See," Jonathan says to Suzanne. "I didn't have to tell them. They figured it out."

"I can't wait for your wedding! I've got a dozen ideas for the cake." Elaine says with a cheerful smile.

With the support of the entire Carmichael family, I can't help but feel silly that I ever doubted Everett. Our mutual feelings were obvious to everyone but us.

"Go on and take her away Ever," Elaine says. "Maybe you'll give my grandchildren another cousin soon."

No one misses her point. Carina giggles even as I try to look innocent. Suzanne's jaw drops and Jonathan wears a sheepish grin as he adjusts his baseball cap.

"Everyone knew?" Suzanne asks.

She looks mildly disgruntled when we collectively nod.

"I'm stealing Sam," Everett says as he guides me with a hand placed on my lower back.

"Bye Sam!" Carina shouts.

"We're not really going on a hike, are we?" I ask in a hushed whisper.

The Carmichaels are close enough to overhear.

"Picnics are romantic," Everett whispers back.

"Ticks, ants, poison ivy, mosquitos..." I trail off as Everett begins to laugh.

"We'll eat at the cabin," he says. "All the outdoor beauty visible through a clear glass window and conveniently located near my bed."

"Smart man," I murmur as he drives us home.

***

The basket lands on his coffee table with a thud. He's not usually careless but his attention is otherwise occupied. My hands slide into his blonde hair to grip the strands at the base giving me leverage to pull his mouth down to mine. Relief and joy mix into a potent storm of emotion that bleeds into our kiss. His hands glide along my body, pulling my shirt up and unhooking my bra without breaking our kiss.

He only pulls away, green eyes dark with desire, to pull my shirt over my head. I don't return the same courtesy. As he returns, his pink lips puffy from our less than gentle kiss, I grab the front of his button down. With one sharp forceful tug his shirt splits down the middle sending buttons flying to all corners of his living room.

The food can wait.

I'm done holding back with this man. He knows me better than anyone else and if he says he loves me I know he loves all of me. There are no hidden shameful secrets between us, only years of friendship and love. It's a race to see who can shed the other's clothes the fastest. Shoes land in corners with one narrowly missing the TV.

"Easy," Everett says a second before he trips.

His khakis tangle around his feet. Off balance from my fumbling attempts to strip him he falls back onto the couch. Staring up at me in surprise he's quick to grab my wrist and tug me down to join him.

"Wouldn't a bed be better?" I ask.

My skin tingles where he traces his lips along the side of my neck. It tickles but more than that it makes me more aware of my body. My nipples harden into points as his warm breath caresses my collarbone. Anticipation paints my body in arousal, making my breath ragged as I nearly whimper from little more than a steamy kiss.

"Next time," Everett replies as his mouth skates down my sternum.

The stubble on his cheeks hits my softest flesh, fire sparking as he moves across my breasts. His tongue strikes out to flick one rosy peak before his lips follow sucking the tip into his mouth. Wet heat engulfs my nipple, the soft tugging sensation sending sparks through my core.

He pushes my pleasure higher even as we continue to scramble to remove our clothing. My jeans might as well be painted on, and we knock elbows as Everett tries to peel them down my legs. Our laughter mingles in the warm living room as we tumble off the couch.

"Should have known you wouldn't make this easy on me," he says.

"Me?" I ask in outrage. "You're the one who decided on the couch."

"Bed, couch, floor. I'll fuck you anywhere Sam," he says his lips a breath away from mine. "I'll take you in the middle of town on the courthouse steps if you want."

"Everett!" I snap.

My hand slaps against his bare chest and I try not to let the firm muscle beneath my palm distract me from the utter ridiculousness of his words.

"Oh, honey," he purrs against my lips. "Do you not want everyone to see how much I want you? How much I crave your delicious little body?"

I'll never admit that the idea of him publicly claiming me turns me on just a little bit.

"My sweet little bride is just a little naughty," he whispers before he presses a kiss to my lips that drips liquid fire.

"Do you have any idea how sweet you taste?" he asks.

I shake my head even as his lips trail down my neck.

"Like honey, fresh and sweet as any bear claw you've ever made me."

The tone shifts as Everett lines himself up with my core. This is a first for both of us, but it doesn't feel clumsy. Every touch, every kiss feels right. It feels like us.

His cock pushes into me slowly, his green eyes searching mine the entire time. I can see the strain on his face as he struggles not to thrust his entire length into me.

"More," I demand when he pauses. "Give me more."

"You want me to just fuck you?" he asks. "Don't you want me to be gentle?"

"Gentle is overrated," I mutter as I shift my hips forcing him to go deeper.

There is a slight sting, and Everett's lips tighten when he notices me wincing. I've wanted this for so long. So many lonely nights letting my imagination create a fantasy that had me dripping as I used my own fingers to bring myself relief. I've got him between my thighs and I'm not letting him slow down now.

"Sam," he groans. "We don't need to rush this. We can take our time."

Letting my thighs fall to the side has him sinking another inch of his cock into me.

"I've been waiting for years," I tell him. "You've cock blocked me for *years*."

His shocked laughter rumbles though his chest down to where we are joined, and the slight vibration is enough to have his shaft bumping against my clit. My moans mingle with his laugh, and I just want him to move already. To stretch me past my breaking point. My body has adjusted to his invasion and there are parts of me yearning for more.

"The blocking was mutual," he says.

Adjusting the angle of my hips I sigh when he slams home. Fullness. Blessed fullness that my fingers alone could never mimic.

"You feel amazing," he whispers.

"Ditto," I gasp. "Now please move."

"Like this?" he asks.

Heat races down my spine as he moves over my body. My body clenches around his cock as he pulls back mourning the loss before he surges back.

"Yes," I moan. "Just like that."

Everett moves at a steady pace creating a rhythm that has me ready to climb the walls. The room falls away as my focus centers on the man who makes me feel safe and on edge simultaneously.

Our bodies slam together with enough force to have me sliding across the hardwood floor with a sharp squeak. I could be annoyed but the way he twists his hips makes me forget everything but the hot press of his cock as he thrusts into me.

I come, squeezing his cock, as the muscles in my arms and legs lock down and my eyes close to find star bursts painted on the lids. My breath comes out in pants as Everett continues to fuck me through the orgasm.

Aftershocks are still rolling through my body leaving me breathless as my body continues to clench around him.

"Sam," he moans. "I-I-"

His seed fills me before he can finish his sentence. The hot sticky liquid coats me from the inside and his last thrust has me coming around his cock again. I milk him for every white pearly drop before he pulls out and slumps to the floor beside me.

"Next time is going to be on a bed," I grumble halfheartedly.

"Definitely," he replies. "My knees are sore."

The next time was in fact not on the bed. Nor the one after that. We made it to the couch once. The kitchen table after that. We didn't fuck on the bed until we were moving my stuff into our cabin and after we both agreed that beds are overrated.

Epilogue

Everett

Five Years Later

"Daddy!" a child shouts and all three of us turn.

Not one of ours. The little girl in a sparkly pink tutu and leggings runs over to Daniel Hart. Me and my brothers turn back to our little family. Tobias and Carina have three kids although Sam and I suspect they'll be announcing their fourth soon enough. Much like Daniel and Lily they want a big family. Not a second later the oldest Carmichael child is demanding to play on the inflatables.

And one where one leads, the rest follow.

Suzanne and Jonathan stopped after one child, little Charlie follows Piper like they're twins and not cousins.

Suzanne no longer runs a delivery route. She has coordinated with Melody Thomas to provide tourists with field guides and a scavenger hunt to identify local wildlife with a focus on moths. Last I heard Jonathan still holds the high score at ninety-five but only because Suzanne isn't allowed to compete.

"Da-ad," my oldest calls out.

I look over to see Evie standing next to her mother. Leaving my brothers to sort out their own broods I join my wife with a smile.

Today is the Crescent Ridge Fire Department's fundraiser and all the local businesses closed early. Hundreds of people are crowding around the fairgrounds with dozens of inflatable slides and obstacle courses, and it is chaotic in the best way. Children are laughing and shouting as they run around with sticky fingers and lips dyed from cotton candy and Kool-Aid.

"How are the twins?" Sam asks even as she reaches out to brush the fine hairs on Samuel's head.

"Sarah was getting a little fussy, but she's settled down."

The twins are strapped to my chest in a baby carrier, the extra weight barely noticeable.

"Mom, you said we could eat once we found dad," Evie pouts.

Looking over at the grill I see Captain Thomas and his wife. He's flipping hamburgers and Melody looks like she's critiquing his technique. The fond smile on his face says it all. The man has been head over heels for his wife since they were kids. He's told all of us the story of how they reconnected after she came back to Crescent Ridge after college more than once.

She's the reason we have a tourist center and even a resort attached to our community now. To hear my mom tell it, Melody saved the town from becoming a slowly dwindling relic.

"I'm starving, let's get some grub," I tell my daughter.

The twins are napping against my chest and when we get our hot dogs and chips, I make sure Sam is seated across from me and Evie at the picnic table. Just like my mom, she takes on too much running the bakery and like my dad I refuse to let her handle everything by herself.

I can feed my daughter. Keeping her stain free is impossible but by the time she's ready to run after Charlie and Piper my wife has finished her food. Not a second after we reach the inflatable slide my mom pops up.

"They've already gotten so big!" she croons.

I shoot an amused look over my mom's head and Sam giggles. The twins are six months old and as the youngest of the grandbabies-for now-they get a lot of attention.

"Do you need me to babysit this weekend?" my mom asks Sam.

"That would be great," she replies. "The Esports league we joined is entering a tournament and we need to get ready."

Mom doesn't have the slightest clue about the video games we play, but she went to every event we played at last year and she's always happy to watch the children.

Between sponsors and prize money, our hobby brings in more money than the bakery or the lumberyard. Neither of us will go full-time for the league though. The bakery is more important to Sam than gaming could ever be and I'm not going to leave my brothers to manage the lumberyard alone. They could handle it, but it's easier for any of us to take time off for our wives and children when there are three of us.

Last winter Piper and Charlie caught the flu together and so did their moms. I was able to handle the lumberyard while Tobias and Jonathan looked after their families.

"We only need a few hours to qualify," Sam whispers in my ear when my mom drifts over to chat with Suzanne.

"A few hours for gaming," I reply. "And a few hours for *other* activities."

"Everett!" Sam cries. "There are children present."

"Oh honey," I purr. "My word choice was delicate just like I'll be-"

Her palm slaps against my mouth muffling my words before I can tell her exactly how I plan to spend our child-free time. The pleased look on her face betrays her excitement. My wife is looking forward to our alone time just as much as I am.

These past five years have brought change but the love we share only grows. Marrying my best friend was the highlight of my life until the birth of our first child, and then the birth of the twins. Each time my heart is full it stretches bigger than I ever thought possible.

"You're welcome," Tobias says.

He joins me watching his three run through the course. He winces when Piper slams into a rounded corner but his daughter bounces back with a laugh.

"What am I thanking you for?" I ask.

"For that horrible acting job that got your ass into gear," he replies. "Sam was never going to send for a husband. She was obsessed with you."

My head tips back and I stare at the blue cloudless sky overhead. I should have known. Sam never mentioned a dating app. Pearl's certainly never came up.

"It was staged," I mutter. "You played me."

"It was Mother's idea," he confides. "You shouldn't be surprised. She had a hand in each of our relationships."

"I'm not. I just can't believe I fell for such an obvious trap."

"Good thing you did," Tobias says bumping my shoulder with his.

Carina and Sam are laughing as the kids barrel past them, sending the women crashing into the sides of the inflatable. I can't imagine what life would be like now if I hadn't taken the leap and went after what I wanted. I like to think I would have made my move eventually.

"Thank you," I say.

"You're welcome," Mom says from beside me.

She grins at me from beside Tobias. I'm not even surprised. My meddling mother is always nearby. Since she retired, she's never too far away from the action. As much as my father likes his quiet days spent restoring old cars, she thrives on managing chaos.

Once she showed up at our cabin with a sandbox, two hundred pounds of sand, and Piper and Charlie in tow. Thankfully, she sent me and Sam down to Bramble for date night. To this day I don't know how she managed to keep all the sand outside the cabin, get the kids cleaned up and in bed by eight. All I know is that when we returned all three of the girls passed out on the living room floor in a pile of blankets and pillows.

The first Carmichael slumber party was a roaring success. As the little kids age up the sleepovers are only going to become crazier.

Watching Sam guide Evie through the obstacle inflatable sends a pang through my chest. The love I felt on our wedding day was magical but the love I feel now makes that feeling seem like a mere shadow in comparison.

I'm married to the woman of my dreams with children I adore and surrounded by friends and family. I wouldn't trade this life for anything. Even if I do have to thank my meddling mother from time to time.

The End

Curious about that no-strings attached kinky sex that brought Emma to Crescent Ridge? Check out Pumpkin Spiced Love, but beware it starts out very NSFW.

Or

If you want more friends to lovers action read A Bride For Dennis. She's his sister's best friend and he's been in love with her for years. He's the boy who grew into a man that makes her want to never leave her hometown.

Printed in Dunstable, United Kingdom